12 Philippine Women Writers

12 Philippine Women Writers

Edited by

Amelia Lapeña-Bonifacio

UNIVERSITY OF THE PHILIPPINES PRESS
Diliman, Quezon City

The Philippine Writers Series, 1994
LIKHAAN: Sentro ng Makathaing Pagsulat
CREATIVE WRITING CENTER
University of the Philippines

Copyright 1994 by the U.P. Creative Writing Center and
the University of the Philippines Press
ISBN 971-542-040-0

First Printing: 1994
Second Printing: 1995

Cover Design: JUNE POTICAR DALISAY
Set in TIMPANI
Book Design and Layout: SYLVIA MENDEZ VENTURA

Distributed outside the Philippines
by the University of Hawaii Press

Printed in the Philippines
by Bookman Printing House

THIS BOOK is lovingly dedicated to WOMEN WRITERS, in my country and all over the world, who have to work doubly hard for recognition; and also,

to WOMEN DOMESTIC HELPERS, in my country and all over the world, who are unable to fight back when maligned, beaten, raped and killed. Wherever they are, for their sake, as well as for the sake of the children and families they left behind, we pray that they will be truly cherished for the services they offer.

PHILIPPINE WRITERS SERIES
LIKHAAN: Sentro ng Makathaing Pagsulat
The CREATIVE WRITING CENTER
University of the Philippines

Table of Contents

Preface *Amelia Lapeña-Bonifacio*	ix
Magnificence *Estrella D. Alfon*	1
Hunger *Gilda Cordero-Fernando*	8
In Time of Moulting Doves *Linda Ty-Casper*	16
The Stairs *Amelia Lapeña-Bonifacio*	26
The Company We Keep *Norma O. Miraflor*	35
Cost Price *Kerima Polotan*	50
The Small Key *Paz Latorena*	59
Love in the Cornhusks *Aida Rivera-Ford*	66
The Lot *Albina P. Fernandez*	72
Grief *Caroline S. Hau*	81

Old Day Today 88
  Edith L. Tiempo
Riverrun 106
  Ninotchka Rosca
The Writers 118

Preface

SOMETIME IN 1986, at the beginning of my term as director of the CREATIVE WRITING CENTER of the University of the Philippines, I made a public statement that before retiring from this position, I would gather in a book some works written by our women writers.

As promised and with the help of the UP CREATIVE WRITING CENTER and the UNIVERSITY OF THE PHILIPPINES PRESS, here is the book. I hope it is not the last for I wish to gather in two other volumes women writers who write fiction in Filipino and writers for children.

These twelve short stories, dating from 1927 to the late 1980s, were chosen from among many beautiful stories written by Philippine women writers in our second language, English. In my selection, I was ruled by two considerations—first, they are told from a woman's point of view and second, they fall into a skein of one continuing yarn—that of a woman's growth from childhood to old age and in the many intervening years between, close to and past her peak years, and of the many concerns that tear her apart or keep her whole.

For who is this creature—mystifying as the moon, strong as a rock and vulnerable as a sapling on a hillside? To the young before their feet can touch the ground, she is the first provider of milk, the first masticator of food, the first keeper of fire at the stove or the hearth, the first mender of clothes and shoes, the first singer of songs and stories, the first teacher of language and manners, the first being to cling to, and be bound to solely, through whose smell commingled with their own she becomes their sole reality, their entire world.

Perhaps it is too presumptuous to say that she can be known through these stories written by women themselves? Who knows, we may find ourselves just a little less confused, if not a little more caring, after reading the fifth or tenth or twelfth story?

ESTRELLA D. ALFON's "Magnificence" is the first story because it establishes her essential role as protector of her young, as fierce as a mother dog that snarls and bites to shield her pup from violators. As that protector, ALFON's mother is Magnificence personified, the terrifying Mother Courage whose punishment is both devastating and just.

GILDA CORDERO-FERNANDO's "Hunger" is an indictment of the neglect suffered by helpless innocents whose greater need transcends the physical. A child with an outstretched hand is an image that must no longer be a part of any society, because it negates all progress and all civilization. CORDERO-FERNANDO's grave picture of this neglect is even more compelling because her girl-child is a true innocent who views her own tragic situation as play.

LINDA T. CASPER's "In Time of Moulting Doves" is a first exposure to one's roots, to one's old hometown, to one's elders whose smell and appearance are closer to things of the earth—humid soil and gnarled branches. CASPER's story is a slow and calculated unfolding of little Lisa's coming face-to-face with the dead and the dying, whose experience of it is a trauma that cannot be erased.

AMELIA LAPEÑA-BONIFACIO's "The Stairs" is a story of the first flow of menstruation, a most frightening experience for a young girl who discovers herself bleeding for the first time. In LAPEÑA-BONIFACIO's story, it is a mystery unexplained and unexplainable to a young innocent whose elders can only wait for this coming so that they can minister the extremest care and love in its accepted ritual of passage.

NORMA O. MIRAFLOR's "The Company We Keep" on the surface appears to be a story of a twenty-year-old woman's awareness of her parents, her brothers and sisters, and her own "dreams of good records, good grades and good boys reserved for her and her friends." But MIRAFLOR's story goes farther when it examines her own growing realization of a retardate brother's worth, a brother who, when he turned twelve, "either nodded or shook his head and never learned to make a wish" in front of his birthday cake.

KERIMA POLOTAN's "Cost Price" is about poverty and what it does to a sensitive woman who is unable to accept "sodden floors, cockroaches and obscenities on the walls" with her lover's "threadbare collar, scuffed shoes, unmended socks, old handkerchief and empty pockets..." In POLOTAN's story, the woman's bitterness is a two-bladed sword cutting both ways, most savagely, the flimsy strands of tenderness and love which bind two human beings.

PAZ LATORENA's "The Small Key" is a young wife's first expression of the strong and overpowering emotion of jealousy. Its power can be destroyed only by fire in the burning of all shreds and evidences of a past love between her husband and his first wife. In LATORENA's quiet narrative, the most important details of the opening of the trunk and the burning of its contents are left to the reader's imagination. In the end there is only, for the young wife, the fever and the fear; and, for the husband, the "smoldering resentment" and the waiting.

AIDA RIVERA-FORD's "Love in the Cornhusks" is the story of a young mother who is momentarily diverted from the care of her child by a love letter. How many young women have been thrilled by the reading in secret of sweet nothings scrawled in a letter by an admirer? RIVERA-FORD's is one such account that also takes up the guilt feeling which accompanies such an illicit thrill and the belief of our women in the concomitant punishment through harm inflicted on a loved one.

ALBINA P. FERNANDEZ's "The Lot" is a story about a most private wish by wives---the ownership of a lot on which someday a small house may be built. Private because the expression of that wish, which is as old and traditional as the caves---this wish for permanency---may upset a husband who is only trying his best. FERNANDEZ shows us this most private wish, how it festers and turns in a woman's soul, changing her view of the man she married and the quiet desperation it brings about.

CAROLINE S. HAU's "Grief" is about life during the war, when a wife whose husband is taken for forced labor by the enemy takes up the full responsibility of providing for her family. HAU's story dramatizes the drudgery of a wife's struggle through the rotating grindstones that grind the beans into soya that produces the bean curd that bounces in the baskets slung on her shoulders while she walks the streets calling out, "Tao-hue, tao-kua, tao-hue!"

EDITH L. TIEMPO's "Old Day Today" is a story about husbands and "issues"---children and grandchildren. But mostly, it is about aging. TIEMPO moves slowly into the phases---she is immersed in sunlight like a plant, she notices the gardener she first saw when he was a child and whose back is turned to her but whose face is now wrinkled. She is jeered as a witch by some boys and, finally, hurt by a branch they had thrown against the fruits of her tree and, coming to, she notices the stars wheeling past, endlessly.

NINOTCHKA ROSCA's "Riverrun" touches on the "shades of a generation" and how these flit by, "thinning away, passing away..." ROSCA's deft handling of time, which is defined by the striking of a clock's chimes, is equated with a woman's quiet and daily chores of cooking and cleaning. When the old woman is finally loosened in a sleep, a deep and final sleep, "she is borne off...to the unchartered bosom of an undiscovered earth."

As these stories attest, these women writers blasted away at barriers set against women during their time. To cite only the first author, ESTRELLA D. ALFON's projection of male perversion against the very young and, in a later story, initiation into sex, have brought about some very strong objections, including a court case.

In passing, it may be pertinent to note how style and the handling of language have changed from the oldest fictionist —Paz Latorena—to the youngest fictionist in this collection—Caroline Hau (Caroline wrote this story in my Creative Writing Class in Fiction). Without exception, however, the stories show great sensitivity in their much too honest exposure of open wounds that hurt, revealing their authors to be the consummate yielders of the craft of short fiction. It is a genre women seem to excel in, perhaps because their thorough familiarity with the minutiae of daily living enables them to encapsulate these details in the brief glimpses allowed in this literary form. It probably has something to do with their motive force—Psyche beloved of Eros, the animating principle.

Being a woman and one of these authors, I believe these twelve stories provide important women's insights into our own life's passages (however brief they may be). I believe these stories are like sudden blasts that sear and burn away prejudices. Whatever may be the world view of us, at times expressed in derision and plain cruelty, I believe these stories that show how we confront the first experiences—and the last—should elevate us to the position, as the Chinese sages say, of rightful holders of the other half of the sky. ✿

AMELIA LAPEÑA-BONIFACIO
University Professor
Director, CREATIVE WRITING CENTER
UNIVERSITY OF THE PHILIPPINES
Diliman, Quezon City

12 Philippine Women Writers

Magnificence

Estrella D. Alfon

THERE WAS nothing to fear, for the man was always so gentle, so kind. At night when the little girl and her brother were bathed in the light of the big shaded bulb that hung over the big study table in the downstairs hall, the man would knock gently on the door, and come in. He would stand for a while just beyond the pool of light, his feet in the circle of illumination, the rest of him in shadow. The little girl and her brother would look up at him where they sat at the big table, their eyes bright in the bright light, and watch him come fully into the light, a dark little man with protuberant lips, his eyes glinting in the light, but his voice soft, his manner slow. He would smell very faintly of sweat and pomade, but the children didn't mind although they did notice, for they waited for him every evening as they sat at their lessons like this. He'd throw his visored cap on the table, and it would fall down with a soft plop, then he'd go around to them, look at the paper on which they were solving a problem or writing down phrases, and he'd nod his head to say one was right, or shake it to say one was wrong.

It was not always that he came. They could remember perhaps two weeks when he remarked to their mother that he had never seen two children looking so smart. The praise had made their mother look over them as they stood around listening to the goings-on at the meeting of the neighborhood association, of which their mother was president. Two children, one a girl of seven, and a boy of eight. They were both very tall for their age, and their legs were the long gangly legs of fine spirited colts. Their mother saw them with eyes that held pride, and then to partly gloss over the material gloating she exhibited, she said to the man, in answer to his praise, But their homework. They're so lazy with them. And the man said, I have nothing to do in the evenings, let me help them. Mother nodded her head and said, If you want to bother yourself. And the thing rested there, and the man came in the evenings therefore, and he helped solve fractions for the boy, and write correct phrases in language for the little girl.

In those days, the rage was for pencils. School children always have rages going at one time or another. Sometimes it is for paper butterflies that are held on sticks, and whirr in the wind. The Japanese bazaars promoted a rage for those. Sometimes it is for little lead toys found in the folded waffles that Japanese confection-makers had such light hands with. At this particular time, it was for pencils. Pencils big but light, in circumference not smaller than a man's thumb. They were unwieldy in a child's hands, but in all schools then, where Japanese bazaars clustered, there were all colors of these pencils selling for very low, but unattainable to a child budgeted at a "baon" of a centavo a day. They were all of five centavos each, and one pencil was not at all what one had ambitions for. In rages, one kept a collection. Four or five pencils, of different colors, to tie with strings near the eraser end, to dangle from one's book-basket, to arouse the envy of the other children who probably possessed less.

Add to the man's gentleness his kindness in knowing a child's desires, his promise that he would give each of them not one pencil, but two. And for the little girl, who he said was very bright and deserved more, he would get the biggest pencil he could find.

And every evening after that the two children would wait for him, watch him come first into the pool of light, watch him bathed in the brightness of the incandescent bulb, and wait eagerly for him to give them the pencils he had promised them.

One evening he did bring them. The evenings of waiting had made them look forward to his final giving, and when they got the pencils they whooped with joy. The little boy had two pencils, one green, one blue. And the little girl had three pencils, two of the same circumference as the little boy's but colored red and yellow. And the third pencil, a jumbo size pencil really, was white, and had been sharpened, and the little girl jumped up and down, and shouted with glee. Until their mother called from down the stairs. What are you shouting about? And they told her, shouting gladly, Vicente, for that was his name. Vicente had brought the pencils he had promised them.

Thank him, their mother called. The little boy smiled and said, Thank you. And the little girl smiled, and said thank you, too. But the man said, Are you not going to kiss me for those pencils? They both came forward, the little girl and the little boy, and they both made to kiss him, but Vicente slapped the boy smartly on his lean hips, and said, Boys do not kiss boys. And the little boy laughed and scampered away, and then ran back and kissed him anyway.

The little girl went up to the man shyly, put her arms about his neck as he crouched to receive her embrace, and kissed him on the cheeks.

The man's arms tightened suddenly about the little girl, until the little girl squirmed out of his arms, and laughed a little breathlessly, disturbed but innocent, looking at the man with a smiling little question of puzzlement.

The next evening, he came around again. All through that day, they had been very proud in school, showing off their brand-new pencils. All the little girls and boys had been envying them. And their mother had finally to tell them to stop talking about pencils, pencils, for now that they had, the boy two, and the girl three, they were asking their mother for money to buy more, so that they could each have five, and three at least in the jumbo size that the little girl's third pencil was. Their mother said, Oh stop it, what will you do with so many pencils, you can only write with one at a time. And the little girl muttered under her breath, I'll ask Vicente for some more. Their mother replied. He's only a bus conductor, don't ask him for too many things. It's a pity. And this observation their mother said to their father, who was eating his evening meal between paragraphs of the book on masonry rites that he was reading. It is a pity, said their mother, People like those, they make friends with people like us, and they feel it is nice to give us gifts, or the children toys and things. You'd think they wouldn't be able to afford it.

The father grunted, and said, The man probably needed a new job, and was softening his way through to him by going at the children like that. And the mother said, No, I don't think so, he's a rather queer young man, I think, he doesn't have many friends, but I have watched him with the children, and he seems to dote on them.

The father grunted again, and did not pay any further attention.

Vicente was earlier than usual that evening. The children immediately put their lessons down, telling him of the envy of their schoolmates, and please, please, would he buy them more pencils?

Vicente said to the little boy, Go and ask if you can let me have a glass of water. And the little boy ran away to comply, saying behind him, But buy as some more pencils, huh, buy us more pencils: and then went up the stairs to their mother.

Vicente held the little girl by the arm, and said gently, Of course I will buy you more pencils, as many as you want.

And the little girl giggled and said, Oh, then I will tell my friends, and they will envy me, for they don't have as many or as pretty.

Vicente took the girl up lightly in his arm, holding her under the armpits, and held her to sit down on his lap and he said, still gently, What are your lessons for tomorrow? And the little girl turned to the paper on the table where she had been writing with the jumbo pencil, and she told him that was her lesson but it was easy. Then go ahead and write, and I will watch you.

Don't hold me on your lap, said the little girl, I am very heavy, you will get very tired.

The man shook his head, and said nothing, but held her on his lap just the same.

The little girl kept squirming, for somehow she felt uncomfortable to be held thus, her mother and father always treated her like a big girl, she was always told never to act like a baby. She looked around at Vicente, interrupting her careful writing to twist around.

His face was all in sweat, and his eyes looked very strange, and indicated to her that she must turn around, attend to the homework she was writing.

But the little girl felt very queer, she didn't know why, all of a sudden she was immensely frightened, and she jumped up away from Vicente's lap.

She stood looking at him, feeling that queer frightened feeling, not knowing what to do. By and by, in a very short while her mother came down the stairs, holding in her hand a glass of zarzaparilla. The little boy followed her. The mother said, I brought you some zarzaparilla, Vicente.

But Vicente had jumped up too as soon as the little girl had jumped from his lap. He snatched at the papers that lay on the table and held them to his stomach, turning away from the mother's coming.

The mother looked at him, stopped in her tracks, and advanced into the light. She had been in shadow. Her voice had been like a bell of safety to the little girl. But now she advanced into the glare of the light that held like a tableau the figures of Vicente holding the little girl's papers to him, and the little girl looking up at him frightenedly, in her eyes dark pools of wonder and fear and question.

The little girl looked at her mother, and saw the beloved face transfigured by some sort of glow. The mother kept coming into the light, and when Vicente made as if to move away into the shadow, she said, very low, but very heavily, Do not move.

She put the glass of soft drink down on the table, where in the light one could watch the little bubbles go up and down in the dark liquid. The mother said to the little boy,

Oscar, finish your lessons. And then turning to the little girl, she said, Come here. The little girl went to her, and the mother knelt down, for she was a tall woman and she said, Turn around. Obediently the little girl turned around, and her mother passed her hands over the little girl's back.

Go upstairs, she said.

The mother's voice was of such a heavy quality and of such awful timbre that the girl could only nod her head, and without looking at Vicente again, she raced up the stairs. The little boy bent over his lessons.

The mother went to the cowering man, and marched him with a glance out of the circle of light that held the little boy. Once in the shadow, she extended her hand, and without any opposition took away the papers that Vicente was holding to himself. She stood there saying nothing as the man fumbled with his hands and with his fingers, and she waited until he had finished. She was going to open her mouth but she glanced at the boy and closed it, and with a look and an inclination of the head, she bade Vicente go up the stairs.

The man said nothing, for she said nothing either. Up the stairs went the man, and the mother followed him behind. When they had reached the upper landing, the woman called down to her son, Son, come up and go to your room.

The little boy did as he was told, asking no questions, for indeed he was feeling sleepy already.

As soon as the boy was gone, the mother turned on Vicente. There was a pause.

Finally, the woman raised her hand, and slapped him full and hard in the face. He retreated down one tread of the stairs with the force of the blow, but the mother followed him. With her other hand she slapped him on the other side of the face again. And so down the stairs they went, the man backwards, his face continually open to the force of the woman's slapping. Alternately she lifted right hand and left hand and made him retreat before her until they reached the bottom landing.

He made no resistance, offered no defense. Before the silence and grimness of her attack he cowered, retreating, until out of his mouth issued something like a whimper.

The mother thus shut his mouth, and with those hard forceful slaps she escorted him right to the door. As soon as the cool air of the free night touched him, he recovered enough to turn away and run, into the shadows that ate him up. The woman looked after him, and closed the doors. She turned out the blazing light over the study table, and went slowly up the stairs.

The little girl watched her mother come up the stairs. She had been witness, watching through the shutters of a window that overlooked the stairs, to the picture of magnificence her mother made as she slapped the man down the stairs and out into the dark night.

When her mother reached her, the woman held her hand out to the child. Always also, with the terrible indelibility that one associates with terror, the girl was to remember the touch of that hand on her shoulder: heavy, kneading at her flesh, the woman herself stricken almost dumb, but her eyes eloquent with the angered fire. She knelt. She felt the little girl's dress and took it off with haste that was almost frantic, tearing at the buttons and imparting a terror to the little girl that almost made her sob. Hush the mother said. Take a bath quickly.

Her mother presided over the bath that the little girl took, scrubbed her, and soaped her, and then wiped her gently all over and changed her into new clothes that smelt with the clean fresh smell of clothes that had hung in the light of the sun. The clothes that she had taken off the little girl, she bundled into a tight wrenched bunch, which she threw into the kitchen range.

Take also the pencils, said the mother to the watching newly bathed, newly changed child. Take them and throw them into the fire. But when the girl turned to comply, the mother said, No, tomorrow will do. And taking the little girl by the hand, she led her to her little girl's bed, made her lie down and tucked the covers gently about her as the girl dropped off into quick slumber. ✿

Hunger

Gilda Cordero-Fernando

"WHO SHALL we be today, Trinity?"
"Mr. and Mrs. Zeppelin, up the hill?"
"No, we've been them so many times before."
"Miss Bartlett, the flute teacher then?"
"I've got an idea, let's be my family for a change," said Trinity, "We've never played a Filipino family yet. And please tuck the dolly in."
"Right-o. I'm Mrs. de Santos and we're having *mee* for lunch."
"Not *mee,* Ching Ling, that's Chinese food... we'll have *sinigang*—it's really fish and tamarinds but a little sand and sunflower seeds will do."
Ching Ling's mother sat rocking in the sun porch in her silk *samfu,* smoking a cigarette and sipping tea from a jade green cup.
"Two tablespoons of sand..."
"And a cup of rain water..."
Outside the window, past the bamboo fence heavy with tiger orchids, the English Mrs. Evans walked down the road in her damp bathing suit, her wet footprints long and thin on the concrete. She carried a faded bag with *Singapore Beach Club* stamped on it. Her freckled arms were caught at the wrists by two Javanese bracelets.

"There goes Wendy's mother," whispered Ching Ling. "Mark my word, Wendy will be around soon enough."

"Yes, I know," said Trinity de Santos. "When Mrs. Evans goes out, Wendy goes out. Shall we hide?"

"Don't you just hate her?"

"Ssshhh..."

"But she's so greedy. Always asking for things to eat in other people's houses. My mother says it's strange because her family's not poor at all."

" 'I could use another piece, ma'am', 'What a lovely pie, ma'am'..." mimicked Ching Ling.

"And her eyes bulging out of their sockets like light bulbs," said Trinity. "Maybe her mother doesn't want to feed her."

"At the school picnic at the Reservoir she finished 56 marshmallows, though she didn't bring anything."

"And remember Mingyoke's party? Where she kept five sticks of *saté babi* under her blouse and they fell when she was pinning the tail on the donkey?" Trinity and Ching Ling screamed with laughter.

"She must be full of tapeworms!"

Wendy Evans walked down the road, the bow of her polka dot dress trailing in the dust. Twelve silver bracelets jingled on her left wrist. She walked with her eyes cast down, hoping she'd find a penny or a safety pin or somethig.

At the intersection, Mustafa, the grocer's boy, pedalled furiously by, an orange-billed mynah cawing on his shoulder. Sometimes it flew above his head, following the trishaw, then alighted again on his shoulder.

Wendy vigorously waved a braceleted hand. "Give me a ride!"

"Get out of the way," screamed Mustafa. "You'll get caught in the wheels."

"Give me a sweet then," said Wendy, laughing and running zigzag in front of Mustafa's trishaw. The grocer's boy reached into the delivery basket and threw a piece of candy into a tuft of grass.

Wendy dived into the grass and found it. It was an after-dinner mint. She sat down under the shade of a rubber tree and unwrapped it. Once upon a time this rubber tree and many other rubber trees made up a jungle and the Sultan of Johore hunted tigers in it. When Papa brought her once to the Sultan's summer place in Penang, she saw all the tiger heads in it. Wendy lay down on her tummy and pretended to be the Sultan of Johore stalking a tiger.

When the candy had melted in her mouth, Wendy looked for the wrapper and licked it. In the distance, past the fringed palm trees and the peaked thatch-roof houses of the Malays, she could see the Chinese cemetery where her mother always went after swimming. Mr. Zeppelin was always meeting her there to teach her how to drive. Wendy's father could teach Mama how to drive but he was always so busy at the Consulate and besides their Mercedes Benz was too new to learn on. They always quarreled about it.

Wendy got up from the grass still licking the candy wrapper, the bow of her polka dot dress dragging after her in the dust. The houses along Wallace Way were drowsing in the sunlight—vine-covered fairytale cottages with industrious people puttering in their gardens and in their kitchens, making taffy and brewing tea. But some were very old, with witches in it. A rotary sprinkler was whirling on Mrs. de Lange's lawn and her ground lilies had burst into bloom — spider-shaped, with flecks of purple. Wendy broke one off and smelled it. It tickled her nose. She wondered if she could give it to Trinity de Santos in exchange for a piece of cake.

Trinity's mother baked such mouth-watering cakes. She used to run a cooking school in Manila until Mr. de Santos decided that saxophonists stood a better chance in Singapore, so now they lived here. Ehem-ing, Wendy wiped her shoes politely at the de Santos door. She saw Mrs. de Santos slipping a sponge cake into the oven and tiptoeing around the kitchen so it wouldn't fall. It wouldn't do to have a sponge cake with fallen arches. The baby in Mrs. de Santos' tummy had grown larger than last time, almost like a watermelon against the edge of the sink where she had tiptoed to wash some lentils for dinner. Wendy sat quietly down on a kitchen stool and sniffed ecstatically. She liked the smell of Mrs. de Lange's kitchen which was wine-y and lemon-y like the Tiffin Room of Raffles Hotel, and the smell of Mrs. Ching's which was spicy and meat-y like the Chicken Inn, and Mrs. Sharma's which was stained with yellow curry like the food stalls of the Esplanade; but best of all she liked Mrs. de Santos' kitchen which smelled of baking all the time. The old oven was all worn from turning out goodies and the tablecloth had a patch on one corner because people were always eating on it, and some of the willowware saucers were chipped. In Wendy's house, the kitchen was spotless and cold like a big igloo—there was a double door refrigerator in it and a tea service cart, and little silver spoons that were used only by company. And the gleaming white range was new but Mrs. Evans never boiled anything on it but water, and if you looked down the sink, it was choked with tea bags.

"Hello, Wendy," said Mrs. de Santos without looking over her shoulder.

"How did you know it was me?" asked Wendy delightedly. "I've got something for you."

"That's very sweet," said Trinity's mother, fingering the spider lily absently and finally tucking it in her apron. She went back to the oven and peeped in.

"Is that a sponge cake you're baking?" asked Wendy, trying to look in too.

"Yes, it is," said Trinity's mother. "Why don't you go down and play at Ching Ling's, Wendy? I don't want my sponge cake falling."

"I'm very careful," said Wendy, slithering as quietly as she could down the kitchen stool. "I bet you never spoiled a cake in your life."

"Oh I did, lots of times."

"What kinds of cake? I mean, what flavor?"

"Oh—strawberry and lemon and chocolate..."

"I just love chocolate, don't you? I bet I could eat a whole mountain of chocolate. Can I watch you frost the cake?"

"I guess so. But now suppose you go to Ching Ling's house and I'll call you when it's ready."

Wendy walked the diagonal short cut to Ching Ling's house, across the tiny marsh that was full of frogs when it rained. She found the girls playing on the porch with Ching Ling's new tea set. Small plates and squares of paper napkin were laid out on a low stool and Trinity was spearing gumdrops on them. "Another helping of *sinigang*?" asked Trinity.

"Surely," said Ching Ling, popping a gumdrop into her mouth and unfolding the square of napkin daintily. "And Wendy," said Ching Ling, her voice like Miss Adey's the ballet teacher, when you couldn't do the first position. "When you see food, you mustn't stare with your eyes bulging like a froggy's—it's bad manners."

"You must pretend to look away," said Trinity. "And when you're asked 'Do you want any,' you must say *no* first."

Wendy looked out the slats of the screen, far away at the Chinese cemetery where her mother was learning how to drive. "How about some gumdrops?" asked Trinity.

"No, thank you," said Wendy.

"All right, if you don't want any then we won't give you any!" shouted Ching Ling and Trinity, popping all the gumdrops in their mouths.

Wendy pulled up the strap of her jumper and shuffled out of the porch. She could hear Trinity and Ching Ling calling her back, but she pretended to have suddenly been struck stone deaf. Near the drainpipe, she found Otto Sandrock's turtle taking a drink of water. Its back was painted white, with a pink O on it. Wendy followed its lumbering path up to Professor Sandrock's backyard. Otto and his friend, Gullygully, were lying on the sand pile drinking soda pops, their new pet snakes slithering around their necks. The other night, Professor Sandrock had accidentally sat on Otto's baby cobra and crushed it to death and Otto's weeping could be heard clear over at Wendy's house. Professor Sandrock had bought a teeter-totter and a straw cap in exchange for it. Professor Sandrock was always loving his children.

"I see you got a new snake, Otto," said Wendy, pressing her forehead against the cool grills of the fence.

"So what's it to you?" Otto finished his soda pop and threw the bottle over the fence. Otto stood on his head against the wall of the house. He turned eight hand-springs. Gully-gully slid the other snake off his neck and put it in a rattan basket. Gully-gully started to walk on his hands. You could see that the seat of his pants was terribly dirty.

Wendy decided to go to the Chinese cemetery to remind her mother that it was lunchtime. The sun was directly over her head, slanting on the gaudy-colored, tallow-encrusted gravestones of the oldest cemetery in Malaya. They said there were so many corpses in it that they had to be buried standing up. Wendy wondered how it felt to be buried standing up.

In front of the moon gate, the strap of Wendy's shoe broke. Wendy sat down on the grass and tried to fix it. She saw her mother backing Mr. Zeppelin's zinc-gray Zephyr in and out between two rows of pebbles, learning how to park. Wendy's mother had thrown a yellow beach towel over her bathing suit. Mr. Zeppelin sat next to her in his Hawaiian shirt, looking like an advertisement in *Punch*. They lurched around the gravestones, trailing clouds of dust.

At the third turn, they saw Wendy by the moon gate, fixing the strap of her shoe. "Don't be following me," said Mrs. Evans, slowing down.

"It's lunchtime, Mama," said Wendy.

"You better go on home then," said Mrs. Evans. "Ayah will take care of you. There's lots of food in the icebox."

Wendy knew there was no food in the icebox but she went on home just the same. She ran down the thick carpet of the igloo, past the piano and the potted palms, her footsteps echoing like muffled heartbeats. In mother's bedroom, she plopped herself down on the quilted seat of the dresser, reached for the telephone among the bottles of perfume and face tissues and dialed a number, holding the receiver close to her ear.

"Hello, Papa?"

"Wendy? What's my little girl been doing with herself all day?"

"Nothing, Papa." She wiggled on the ruffled stool. "I called up to remind you..."

"Look, sweetheart, there are some people in Papa's office right now... *Important* people..."

"I just wanted to know, Papa, what time we're going..."

"Yes, Wendy?"

"...we're going to Happy World to see the midgets and the tumblers."

"Well, as I was telling you, I'm terribly tied up today... ambassadors, you know... what about tomorrow, or the day after... yes, I *know* I promised... let's talk about it as soon as I get home, shall we?"

"All right, papa."

"Don't cry, Wendy."

The line went dead. Wendy put the receiver back on its cradle. Vaguely, she hunted on the magazine rack for a paper doll or a bit of rag to cut, but there wasn't anything. Wasn't anything at all to cut, or hold or fondle. Her tummy began to hurt. She ran to the window and pressed it hard on the sill. That way it didn't hurt too much. In the yard, Ayah was hanging up the wash, her surly mouth full of clothespins. She looked like somebody's stepmother. Wendy jumped down to the floor and ran to the kitchen.

She jerked open the refrigerator door. There was a bottle of sun tan lotion and an orchid in it. The belly of the ice compartment was fat with ice. Wendy took a knife from the kitchen drawer and scraped some of the "snow" into her tongue. She pretended to be Oona, the Eskimo girl from Alaska, getting a mouthful of storm.

Then Wendy walked out into the yard banging the kitchen door. She stood for a moment looking down at the broken strap of her shoe, wondering where to go. She took the diagonal short cut to Trinity's house to see about the sponge cake but the door was locked. All over the row of houses on Wallace Way, families were having lunch, the sound of their forks and knives and dinner conversation floating down from the curtained windows.

In the cool interior of the de Santos garage, she found the Morris Minor parked. It had three holes in its shiny dome because the day it was bought was the first day of the student riot. Sitting on the fender, Ahmad, the Malayan driver of the de Santos', was having his dinner of bread and salted eggs from a split paper bag. He was a Moslem and he never ate pork, refused to eat from the plates Mrs. de Santos brought out to him because they had touched pork, refused to eat in the kitchen which was sinful with the aroma of pork fat. Ahmad ate the last of the red egg and wrapped up the broken shells. Wendy sighed.

A beggar came down the intersection, walking crab-like, his wasted legs knocking together at the knees. Wendy giggled. He was a queer sight in his ragged *batik* pants, holding a twitching palsied hand out for alms. Under his ragged straw hat, the beggar scanned the road for policemen; many times he had been collared for loitering around the markets of Bukit Timah and Paso Panjang.

The beggar walked past the papaya trees and stopped in front of the kitchen. Wendy saw Mr. de Santos shut the door in the beggar's face. She could hear him quarreling with Mrs. de Santos inside.

"You didn't have to be so harsh," Mrs. de Santos was saying. "He was just asking for some alms."

It's our civic duty to discourage parasitism of any kind," said Mr. de Santos, turning on the faucet and washing his hands off the affair.

"That's all very fine in theory," said Mrs. de Santos querulously. "But when people don't have enough money, or food, or love, they have to beg."

Wendy followed the retreating beggar. She began to mimic him, pushing her legs inward till the knees knocked together, and her empty stomach filled with the gas of her laughter. Stepping crab-wise, laboriously, she stretched her twitching palm out in the age-old gesture of supplication. ✿

In Time of Moulting Doves

Linda Ty-Casper

HOPING TO get seasick, Lisa caught the ship's railing under her lowest rib and, flattening forward, stared off the stern at the waters being torn into stitches and streamers. She had heard the captain tell her mother to look far out at the unmoving blue islands to keep from being sick; but although her mother had been propped up in preparation on her deck-cot, she was sick just the same. So were most of the passengers: they groaned, each from his own cot, over the sound of the diesels. Probably, even the pigs in the ship's hold were sick; at least they had stopped squealing. Half in defiance, half in surrender, Lisa lowered a white flag of spit into the ship's wake. Only *she* was not being cared for.

When she wiped her mouth on her sleeves, the handkerchief pinned to her dress for that purpose scratched her chin. The Friday handkerchief, according to its embroidered ear. Almost hopefully, she looked behind her but nobody had seen her act of outrage. Against the gangway to the lower deck of the inter-islander, she caught the silhouette of her father's masculine ears, like outriggers, and, humbled, she wondered why hers were pinched back so.

Standing beside two big baskets of mango, her father was telling her mother about the river of quicksand where they used to hunt. For nearly eighteen years he had not visited his town in Samar: only two years before Lina's birth, but nine before Lisa's. Anyway, there was nothing in his town for little girls, except crocodiles in the river. She missed Manila already.

Why were there no ocean crocodiles? she wondered. A dark lump appeared in the water. She threw a loosened button at it because it was not a crocodile: it had no big open happy hungry mouth.

"Father, why are there no...?" she shouted from her perch.

"Shhh," her mother looked around, making the face reserved for children (but this morning the cheeks looked gray). When Lisa jumped from the railing, her mother's limp plump arms held her off the cots.

"Does salt water pickle them if...?"

"Go ask Lina."

Lisa kicked the basket of mangoes and, dragging her heels, pulled her mother's slippers to where Lina sat. She flounced her eyes backwards once, but her mother had not even bothered to notice.

Nor did Lina glance sideways to acknowledge her approach. The other girl, in a red dress, now and then rolled into Lina's lap one of the orange-ripe *siniguelas* she was sorting. Lina wiped them on her dress before biting them. Between words, she tilted back her sunburned nose to let the sweet juice flush her throat. "You are only two children?" the other girl was asking. "We're eight."

"That's fun," Lina sucked the big *siniguelas* seed. "I wish I had brothers, too, to dance with."

Lisa tugged at her sister's skirt, hoping that Lina would share the fruits with her, but all she got was a whispered, "Go away." More than ever she wished Lisa were her *sister's* name: she would call her lizard.

"Is that your sister?"

"Yes, look at her hair. You'd think she's moulting. No, Norma?"

Norma laughed deep down in her throat. In that moment, all the shame of the day before---her choking at the table, her spitting crumbs till her mother had to lead her away;

her falling from her cot during the night and the passengers grumbling at her cry—flowed back with the blood to Lisa's face; and she pounded at Lina's calves until her knuckles ached.

"I'm sick! I want ice!" she whimpered, slumping beside Lina. Whenever Lina pulled her up, she slipped back like a dead-weight sack of rice.

"Don't mind her," Norma said. "If she's really sick, ice will only make her sicker. She's pretending so we'll notice her. She'll keep acting till she *really* gets sick. Don't I see it everyday in my little sisters? It's a stage."

But Lisa only groaned louder and Lina dragged her across the deck to the cots.

"Yes now," the waiter with the cup of cracked ice laughed over her. "Ice *is* good—for growing girls!"

Slowly Lisa gnawed the wedge of ice and, covering her head with a pillow, pretended she was an iceberg floating in the North Pole, all submerged except one eye, and all alone.

"Eat your egg," her mother, slipping her belt out one more notch, whispered to Lisa before standing up. "We're almost there. What's wrong with it?"

Lisa gloomily watched the soft-boiled egg unwind from the toothpick with which her mother had taken it from the shell. She was wondering how eggs turn to chickens and where the feathers come from. A real chick—feathers, insides and all—stuck in her throat! She would never eat another egg.

"What are you, Lisa?" Lina pinched her arm. "You're the only one left."

Samar was only a thumb's length off. Even with one eye closed, Lisa could see it; but she could not decide whether it was the ship or the island that was moving faster. Anyway, the collision, she hoped, would come soon.

"Stay with me," her mother jerked her back from the railing. "Is my powder all right, Leon?"

Lisa watched her father's nose twitch approvingly. Why had she missed getting a fine high nose like his?

"Ooooop!" A twist of hemp caught the posts of the landing.

Samar was there, sand-gray houses raised just out of the hug of the shore. The air seemed to be breathed itself.

Lisa ran loose, clutching her mother's silver bag, given to make her come without screaming.

"There's Man Peping," her father's now-husky voice slowed her. Then she felt the man's spread of beard measuring her face. All the way to Calbiga, her cheeks still blistered.

The road cranked its way up the noisy mountain: and Lina kept saying how *beautiful* the view was of the sea; how *beautiful* the trees were; how *beautiful* this and that. Lisa plugged her ears but watched for the first glint of river.

In town, as they went from house to house, she bore at least two more bearded uncles: and a dent started in her forehead from kissing so many hands. From each house she got handfuls of *pili* sweets and the special multi-colored *ampao* which, like a pack-rat, she stuffed in her father's pockets.

(This is my eldest: Lina.—How *beautiful*, like your wife! And this is your other one, the younger?—Yes; Lisa.—Whom does she resemble?—I don't know, exactly. She looks like herself.—Now, Lisa, recite a poem.—She's only nine years old and already in grade four?—The one about the gentleman. Stand straight.)

"I knew him for a gentleman; his coat was thin and rather worn..."

(Probably she's too young yet to look like anyone, Leon.—Never mind, Lisa, don't finish it any more.—Ha, ha, ha, your husband was the best catch around here, before he left. He looked just like his father, all forehead and very clever. Why has it been so many years?)

Lisa pouted. They knew she couldn't understand Visayan, yet they kept talking it and asking if she could. She refused to recite another line. They don't listen anyway, she cried.

(The man who had turned to *tuba* and raw shrimps in onion sauce, laughed: Fill up on candies, Lisa.—I want to go home.—Baby, don't you want to stay with us? Tomorrow is the fiesta.—I don't like.—How can you go home? Can you walk on water?—Why not?—She's spoiled, no?—What *do* you want?—Crocodiles.)

Finally, after sitting down to about six dinners, with the same food—foot-long crabs, large shrimps, broiled milkfish, leche flan—Lisa refused to budge.

"Just one house more," her father coaxed, reaching for his coat.

"The old woman cared for your father when he was orphaned," Man Peping's words seemed stuck to the longest stubble of beard and the most blackened far-apart teeth. "She's the one he must not have forgotten. She always said she'd like to see you once more, Leon. She's blind now."

Although the house was big, it looked unused. There were no chairs, no tables in the living room. Nothing to stumble over. The old woman's washed-white hair looked like dove wings on her head, making Lisa think of the morning flight of their own doves at home. The old woman held her hand awhile and felt about her head.

"I am glad you're here, Leon," she said; and Lisa, to escape those bony fingers, looked up at her father. But his red eyes only bothered her more.

The house across the street was where they would stay.

Inside, Lisa jumped on the bed beside the window and discovered that the room was just above the stairs. Already about four other girls and six boys, Lina's age—and one guitar—were waiting to take them boating to the fields.

"Where are the crocodiles?" Lisa was asking as soon as they boarded the boat, testing the water with her little finger. "There, there behind you!" Fred, the boy in striped shirt, made a panic of eyes and shouted. Everybody thought he was so funny that Lisa was obliged to rock the boat to frighten him; but she was ignored all the way to the landing.

There was one hill, of bamboo shoots and blue-beaked orioles, to cross before they reached the fields where, at last, they munched sugar cane and sang, "*Ay, ay Kalisud.*" Lisa had wanted the cane cut into finger lengths, but finally had to be satisfied with clutching a large piece in her fist and gnawing at it, like the others.

By four o'clock, rain was filtering through the bamboo leaves. "Let's go to the dance early," braided Rosie sing-songed. "You dress fast, Lina."

"I knew him for a gentleman; His coat was thin..."

"Sssh," Lina pinched Lisa's nose. "Don't sing so loud: you're off-key."

"I wasn't singing!" Lisa protected her ears against the laughter. "I'll go home now."

Lisa grabbed an umbrella and refused to share it, because she had never in her life had one all to herself. All the way, she held the umbrella with its ribs just above her head so she could see only the legs flecked with mud.

Later, while Mana Ines who owned the house kept turning Lina around before the sala mirror, Lisa runned her heels sore on the bedpost. Then hearing voices downstairs at last, she looked out. Fred, when he saw her, began a mock serenade, strumming his chestbones.

Flat on the sill, Lisa spat down on Fred's pomaded head. As soon as he looked up, surprised, she jumped back out of sight and hugged herself.

Once outside the church, the saints on their carriages shone like coins heel-dug into sand. But in the late afternoon light their clothes looked unwashed.

The dent in Lisa's forehead was back. Everyone in the churchyard was an uncle, aunt, grandmother met all over again. Old people's talk never ended, and their hands felt like turtles'. Quickly she turned her head to keep from seeing Lina primping and talking with her own friends. Only she was alone, alone, alone. And when would her hair be long enough for *triboson*?

In the churchyard *a las cuatro* plants were fenced with bamboo. How elegant the blood-red flowers would look, planted in her white-eyelet dress! Hurriedly she began to pick-stick them through the eye holes, from neck to knee. Now, she would be more ornamental than Lina. But her pride was scalded when her mother brushed the flowers away in a red, cascade, muttering, "You'll be stained! Look at yourself!"

Lisa, alone again, drifted towards a single white shed behind the church. Nearer the shed, the grass grew up to her skirt, making her legs itch. She tried to part them with her hands and flatten them with her feet. If she went back, they would say she was afraid of snakes. Let her be bitten then, so that they would feel sorry. Then they might finally realize their neglect.

Inside the shed, on a long unplaned table, was a skull. She had never seen one before, except on bottles put out of reach in the bathroom. But this one was not white. There were discolored blotches as if from skin disease, even if there was no more skin. Worms of fear crawled down her legs and left her sticking to the ground. The sun had dropped from the clouds and, flattened on the mountains, gleamed hard and red; its light drew her eyes around in a circle. Downhill, just a few feet off, was a slope of crosses.

The long walk back home, although it kept getting cooler, made her stop shivering.

The churchyard was still crowded. "Did you fall into the open graves?" a fat aunt asked.

They had looked like mouths, the crosses like teeth: Lisa no longer wanted to think of crocodiles. She ran to her father and hugged his leg.

Walking from church, she wondered why everybody was smiling, as if their mouths would never close, despite the crosses among the grass. Whose aunt or uncle was the skull?

Two houses from church, they stopped. As they went up a long wooden stairs, a woman in black waved from the window and, a moment later, carefully lifting her slippers, accompanied them inside the rubbed cheeks with Lisa's mother. In the living room, the chairs lined against the walls were filled, the trays of food and drink were emptied. Near the windows where curtains, still creased from being folded, were hanging windless, men in clusters of white suits sat apart from their wives in chicken-colored gowns.

Intense light, flickering and multiple, glowed coldly from an open door. Tagging after her father, Lisa entered the room where wailing made even the gas-lights quiver. On the bed was a dead old woman.

Lisa tried to pull her father from the relatives who, their faces sobering as they entered, placing cigar or fan behind them, took turns kissing the dead woman's hand, lined and veined at her side. Under his breath her father said, in a watery voice, "Lola, Lola...."

The feet that showed beneath the skirt might move at any moment. Vaguely she remembered hearing of dead people who stood up in their coffins. Here, no coffin would hold the old woman back, would keep her from chasing whoever might not kiss her hand.

"Let's leave now, Father," she cried. Earnestly she wiggled her toes inside her shoes, afraid that she would have to put her lips against those cold bones also. "I will not! I won't!"

"Stop acting," Lina poked her back.

She closed her eyes. She would never look at a dead person again.

They were near the body now, she could tell by her sliding feet. Suppose *her* eyes opened, and faced Lisa! They drew nearer, until she could smell the odor of death like thickened wax. The scream shriveled through her lips at last; her knee touched the bed.

The maid, muttering in Visayan, dragged her down the flight of trembling wooden stairs. Lisa stumbled but dared not look back at the big house. She had even refused to eat at the table, because a hundred blackened doors lined the dining room and she kept looking around, waiting for the dead woman to come out of each one.

Her tongue curled, as if she had just licked a piece of metal.

Candles and gas lamps lit the windows of all the houses, as if each one celebrated a funeral, not a fiesta. From the church rose a slow careful chant. Bending forward, men stood ready to pull the carriages past the people standing with arm long candles. The procession had begun.

"Don't," Lisa yelled as the maid stopped to watch, "Let's go home." She pulled and kicked. To her, the saints surrounded by candles till their faces lengthened were as dead as the woman on the bed. It was another funeral.

Once at home she dropped into bed and stiffened her arms when the maid pulled off her dress. Shaking her head at the pajamas, she asked for her nightgown. Each time the maid turned her back, Lisa twitched her nose. She was happy now, with somebody taking care of her at last. She felt drenched, though she was not sure with *what*.

"Stay with me even when I sleep," she told the maid who stood on one leg in the doorway, frowning.

With the light blanket over her head she felt safe. Even the funeral candles could not drop their wax on her.

Her leg gave a sudden start: the earth had turned a corner and she was alone in her room. What was the maid's name? Angrily, when the blood returned, she slipped her legs out of bed.

The sala was one endless candle light, but at least the shadows were pushed, now, under the chairs and tables. She tried to take back her thoughts from the dead woman and to think instead of the carnival before school closed, of the folk dancing. But the clown's black dress, the candle at the dance, were reminders of the bedside and the many waiting doors.

To prove to herself that she was fearless, Lisa walked to the middle of the room, eyes on the table's candy jar. Table edge against her ribs, her hand was already out when, feeling watched, she stopped. Darkness was staring in at the window.

"Father," she shouted. "Father!" The cry withered her face, making it old, she felt. Several times she shouted but only the far-off chants of the procession answered.

Still alive, she looked around, through the open porch door, and saw the blind old woman they had visited, squatting at the foot of the stairs in the other house.

The old blind woman too had been left, was alone. And without eyes. Was she frightened of the darkness inside her? She wore the same faded grassy skirt she had worn the day before. Had she no new clothes? What did she *own*; what kep her company during her hours of waiting? Lisa thought of old beggars with chins trembling and eyes slashed by the sun. Now the hair, wing-white, seemed blown, seemed disturbed but brave. "She's moulting," Lisa thought, but did not think of laughing.

She would have run down to the old woman, had the fear not come back as she turned. Again she was caught, stuck to the floorboards.

The smell of wax nearly drowned her as she peered through the porch railing at the blind old woman. "Lola, Lola..." she whispered, like a chant, "Lola..." ✿

The Stairs

Amelia Lapeña-Bonifacio

IT WAS a sharp pain, a hard nut of pain which throbbed in the pit of her belly, different from any pain she had ever experienced before. Ligaya was jumping *piko* when she felt it and for a moment, she thought she would faint and fall on the hard ground marked with the half-moon of the boxed patterns and the flat stones of their game.

Diwata and the other girl sat under the shade of the *ipil-ipil*, waiting for their turn. "Is something wrong?" they asked almost in unison.

"No, nothing—nothing's wrong," Ligaya said, the hard nut now seemed to whirl, pulling every muscle of her stomach into a taut vortex until her belly felt rigid as a tin plate.

"Well, what are you waiting for then?" Diwata asked her quite sharply.

"It's nothing, stupid," Ligaya snapped back. "I'm just plotting my next move as you can see."

"You can't take all day, like a queen," the girl, whose braids smelled of rancid coconut oil, ventured, her thick Visayan accent prolonging the last word. To Ligaya, she was a no-name, a newcomer of their village where her family had come to settle as farmhands after a long sea voyage from the Visayas. She was a stranger and her words stung. The girl was squinting under the hot afternoon sun, toying with her braids as she regarded Ligaya at the center of the unevenly drawn half-moon.

Ligaya approached the girl with deliberate steps and hovered over her, her arms akimbo. "You go back to where you came from if you don't like the way we play here!" No-name's hand fell from her braids to snatch her wooden clogs from the hard ground. She hugged them to her thin chest, the brightly-painted red clogs, raised her rear, as if set to race.

"Well, well," Diwata broke in, "it's just a game where some people must win and some people must lose. You've captured so many houses already, so why are you so greedy?"

Ligaya looked at the two, then walked away from the half-moon into the shade, slumping against the tree. "Well," she said, "well, if some people here can't wait, they can just go on without me. I'm tired of it anyway." The pain started to throb again, she pressed her palm against it to stop the ache.

"Suit yourself," Diwata said getting to her feet. "If some people think they can stop this game by quitting, ha!" By this time, she was in front of Ligaya, her dusty feet kicking up a clumsy dance to taunt her.

"You know what, you know what," she chanted, "some people here will see how we will split her houses! Split her houses!"

"That'll make mine four houses all in all," No-name said, smiling up at Diwata.

"Now, all we do is decide who'll play first," Diwata said, extending her clenched fist to No-name. "Take three."

No-name spat into her palms and clenching one of them, offered it solemnly to Diwata. Their fists met on an imaginary line in the accepted preliminaries of the game. Twice they each swung their arms in abrupt gestures, intoning in sing-song,

"Jack and Poy, *holi, holi, hoy!*"

And twice their arms rose and fell as they stomped their feet on the hard ground.

"My paper to wrap your stone," cried Diwata gaily, open palm against No-name's clenched fist.

Ligaya tore off the blades of grass growing around the base of the *ipil-ipil*. It was so hot even in the shade and there were the two of them in quiet concentration, fighting over her houses.

"Scissors will cut your paper," shouted No-name, "That's one for me!"

She chewed the tender shoots and spat out the bitter taste. Suddenly, she could no longer wait to see who was the winner. In an instant, Ligaya was up, running to the boxes marked "L" and before they could stop her, she was dragging her feet over her initials.

"You're both stupid," she cried. "You didn't even work for my houses, they're mine. Mine!" She dug her heels into the ground where a pointed stick had etched her initial. "Start all over again," she cried, making arch movements with her bare foot and raising a cloud of dust as she went on, determined to erase all her houses.

"What did you do that for?" It was Diwata who broke away from No-name and was suddenly beside her. "You're no longer in the game!"

Ligaya shrugged her shoulder and continued with her task.

Diwata said evenly, "You'll stop that this instant!"

But Ligaya kept on swinging her leg. "Make me," she said.

"You're out of the game," cried Diwata. Before she could duck, Diwata had pounced on her and they fell on the hot dust. In a second, No-name jumped into the fight, the two of them pinning her down. Ligaya felt her hair being tugged at, by Diwata or No-name, she could not tell although she saw how their faces shone with sweat, their hard breathing drowning her own.

"Say you give up!" No-name demanded, applying the full pressure of her palm against Ligaya's face on the hot dust. She felt Diwata twisting her leg. Ligaya lifted her head from under No-name's palm in order to answer, when suddenly, she felt Diwata releasing her hold. No-name removed her palm also.

"Why, Gaya, your dress!" Diwata sounded greatly alarmed.

No-name started to whimper. "We didn't mean to kill you," she said, leaving a streak of grime on her face as she wiped her nose with the back of her dusty hand. They both stood up, looking down on her.

"What's wrong?" Ligaya said jumping on her feet.

"We didn't mean to hit so hard," Diwata apologized.

"But you asked for it," No-name said, hiding behind Diwata.

"You can join the game again, if you want to..." Diwata offered.

"She'll have to see the doctor first," No-name suggested. "Meantime, let's split her houses until she comes back."

Ligaya paid no attention to them. She passed her hand over her forehead, examined her dusty arms and legs. Except for a few bruises, they looked all right.

"Look at your skirt," they said.

Ligaya twisted her cotton skirt and shrieked when she saw the blotted hem. Her first instinct was to run. She backed away from them, gathering up her skirt and twisting the soiled portion of it into a tight ball.

"Tell your mother we didn't do it or else...," No-name advised her.

Diwata looked at her quietly. Ligaya turned away from them and sped off, her hand still clutching the balled hem of her skirt. The trees and the thatched roofs floated above her and still higher, the blue strip of sky fled with her. She could feel the wind and the hot sun against her feverish face. From one or two windows, faces stuck out to look at her racing in the afternoon sun. As she turned the corner of the last hut before her house, a boy leading a carabao by a broken rope knotted through its nostrils shouted after her, "Hoy *bata batuta*, where's the fire, hah!" Then he laughed derisively, his laughter following her to their backyard.

Ligaya slackened her pace when she reached their backyard. The backdoor was open. Her mother would be dozing off in her regular siesta on the bamboo *papag* in the kitchen, her graying hair loosened from its tight knot and spread over the heavily-starched, embroidered pillow. Ligaya held her breath as she entered the house on tiptoe. She was almost at the foot of the stairs when her mother's sleepy voice called out to her.

"Is it you, Gaya?"

"Yes, it's only me, *Inang*," Ligaya answered.

"Come and lie down beside me, *anak*," she said in the same sleepy voice.

"But I don't feel sleepy, *Inang*, not at all," Ligaya said.

"Then you can comb my hair and look for whites? They itch so."

"Later, *Inang*," she said, quickly climbing the bamboo stairs.

"Five whites for a centavo?" she coaxed.

Ligaya stopped. That was better than the seven she always insisted upon. But she said, "Later *na lang, Inang*, I'll be back..."

Ligaya ran up the stairs. Up where it was bright with the afternoon sunlight, the *sawale* windows had been pushed wide open and the sun spilled on the rocking chairs, the shiny tea table and the split bamboo floor. She ran to the little room where they kept the family's blankets, pillows, rolled mats and trunks of clothes. It was a small rectangular enclosed area which was dark because it did not have any windows. Just a tiny half-door. With a sigh of relief, she sat against the pillows and neatly stacked blankets reaching halfway to the slant of the low thatched roof. It was nice to hide there as she had done many times. The pillows smelled of starch and fragrant banana leaves which her *Inang* used to slide the hot iron on before pressing the clothes. She pulled a greenish woolen blanket and covered herself carefully, pulling the hem to her chin. There was the pain again. She was going to die, she thought. Somehow, her life was being drained away from her by some unknown and mysterious force. It happened many times before in the village. When one makes the mistake of insulting the *aswang* or *mangkukulam*, whether one did it willfully or not, they turn into malevolent spirits driven to revengeful rage so that there was no telling what they would be up to. She thought hard on who she might have insulted. Last week, the neighbor's baby died for no apparent reason. She heard the woman next door whispering it was surely the *aswang* that did it with its long tongue which can take on the appearance of a thread innocently lying on the floor, but in truth it was a tongue waiting out there to suck in an innocent human's liver! She shuddered and tried to shake it off her mind but her eyes sought the floor for any telltale piece of thread. She was happy to find none.

The sun was a red-orange ball which blinked at her through the slits of the thatched wall. In the center of the yard, she could see the *madre de cacao* in full bloom, its tiny soft lavender blossoms transparent against the afternoon sun. Gradually, the sun seemed to dip behind the hills and because she watched it for a long time, her eyes held its bright red ball against the sky of gold even after it was gone. She closed her eyes and the red ball turned into a black circle which bobbed crazily in her teary vision. Then everything turned into a soft murkiness in the warmth of her green blanket cocoon.

Laughter broke the soft darkness, men laughing and water splashing as the rusty artesian pump was being cranked. "Whoa, big boy, whoa," it was her *Itang*'s voice. She rubbed her eyes. They were home already, her brother's laughter drifted up to her hiding place. They were washing their plows, the carabaos and their muddy arms and legs. It must be suppertime and they would be looking for her!

But her sister Mely found her soon enough. She had just turned on the low-hanging bulb in the tiny room and was getting some towels from the trunk when she saw Ligaya.

"Hoy, what are you doing there, little monkey?" she said.

Ligaya drew the blanket closer to her chin. "I like it here," she said.

"*Inang* is looking for you," Mely said draping two or three towels over her shoulder. She pressed down the lid of the trunk until the latch clicked close.

"She knows I'm here," Ligaya said.

"Gaya, come and help set the table or *Inang* will be angry...."

"I don't feel too well," Ligaya said.

"Are you sick?" With this, her sister's cool palm cupped over her brow. "Come for a bowl of hot soup then, *Inang* will give you some and then you'll feel much better."

"I'd rather stay here," Ligaya said.

"I've had enough of your tricks, Gaya, you're not sick, you just don't want to help so why not just so!" Mely yanked away her green blanket cocoon in one swift move. It was all too sudden, Ligaya shivered visibly, hid her face in her arms and started to cry.

Her sister replaced the blanket gently, turned off the light and left the room hastily. When Ligaya could wipe away her tears and bend over to peek through the slits of the bamboo floor, she saw her sister holding an excited conversation with *Inang* and *Tia* Waya, a spinster aunt. She saw her father being told while her brothers stood around rubbing the water from their hair with the towels Mely had handed out to them.

"But she's only a child," Ligaya heard *Itang* protest.

"Well, she's almost twelve," *Inang* told him quietly.

"There's no stopping these things," *Tia* Waya said, shaking her head a bit too mournfully.

Itang walked to the bright stoves where supper was cooking. The flames flickered against the shape of his head. He drew out one of the burning pieces of wood from under the clay pot and lighted his cigar, drawing heavy puffs of smoke around them. *Inang* had followed and she stood behind him, waiting.

"Well," *Itang* said, still sucking in some air, the tip of his cigar aglow, "well, it's your job, you know."

"Yes, of course, I suppose it is," *Inang* said.

Ligaya turned back to the pillows and hid her face. Strangely enough, she was still alive, considering it was evening already. And the pain seemed to have disappeared. She felt a little weak and somewhat depressed, otherwise everything seemed as it was before.

When she heard the bamboo stairs creak and she saw them enter the half-door, Ligaya pulled the blanket tightly about her. In the soft darkness, she could see *Inang*'s bent figure, behind her was *Tia* Waya with some folded cotton napkins draped on her arm.

"Nothing's wrong, *anak*," *Inang*'s voice was gentle as she placed a basin of water near Ligaya. Ligaya looked up at her with frightened eyes, thankful it was dark in the room. *Inang* started to stroke her head tenderly, murmuring little endearments. Suddenly, Ligaya released her blanket cocoon and flung her arms about her *Inang*'s neck, sobbing while she buried her face in the soft, sweet-smelling white blouse *Inang* wore. When her sobs subsided, they cleaned her, not bothering to turn on the light. Both of them were tender and they did not speak a word. Ligaya submitted herself meekly to their ministrations, permitting herself to be washed and bound, pinned up and clothed.

It was after all the supper things had been removed from the table and washed and the stoves had been brushed until only a thin bed of warm ashes remained for the cats to sleep on, after *Itang* and her brothers vanished off to the *municipio* to see their friends, that *Inang* instructed them to sit around facing the stairs. Her sister Mely took the small black stool and sat near the stairs while *Tia* Waya sat on the bench, her back leaning against the dining table. *Inang* was busy setting up a clay pot filled to the brim with water on which a tin can floated.

Inang turned to Ligaya. "Now do as I tell you, *anak*."

Ligaya hesitated but *Inang* held her by the hand and led her to the stairs. "Now, climb to the fourth rung, *anak*," she said.

"So it'll last no more than four days," said her sister Mely, smiling knowingly.

"Some people here don't know when to remain quiet," said *Tia* Waya.

Ligaya climbed the stairs slowly and sat on the fourth rung, not knowing quite what to do. Her knees felt wobbly.

"Now, listen, *anak*," *Inang* said slowly, "I'll count to three and then you jump about here," she was pointing to a spot near the jar.

The faces watching her below were indistinct under the single lamp hanging behind their back. Ligaya got up on her feet, wavered on the smooth curve of the bamboo step and then raised her arms as if getting ready to dive.

"Ready?" *Inang* had dipped the tin can into the jar and filled it full of water.

Ligaya nodded.

"One—two—," came *Inang*'s slow count, "—three, JUMP!"

Ligaya jumped and was met with a splashful of water from the tin can and then another. Her clothes were drenched and she stood shivering as the three women surrounded her and held her up, all three of them were talking at the same time. For a moment, Ligaya felt the water dripping around her legs, all cool and nice but inside she could feel the strange new warm flow and she did not quite know whether to laugh in relief or to cry in distress.✿

The Company We Keep

Norma O. Miraflor

WE HAD the green chevy parked under the shade of an acacia and because we had to wait long, I had enough time to examine the bark that faithfully bore the marks left by youth and ennui. There were a lot of arrows and a profusion of names inscribed in irregularly-cut hearts and some pen knife had slashed a big 'r' and, for want of something to say, I suggested that this must have been done by some nut I had jilted but the suggestion hurt my throat because, of course, in the heat of summer, nobody found the remark amusing. My brother Chito complained it was stifling, this heat is impossible, I heard him say but I thought he was just talking to the driver so I kept on tapping my fingers lightly on the car seat. Carmita had a very bad cold and she sneezed a number of times and I told her that she should have worn one of those loose easy blouses but she only blinked and sneezed. When our parents came out of the building, it was almost noon and the heat hurt our skin but we felt no need for lunch and we only squirmed in our seats. We knew it would take long, that there were papers to sign and accommodations to make and deposits to pay but it was still a long wait and I straightened my back and yawned.

They walked fast and we watched them cross the yard where a sprinkling of men in loose white garments walked about and gathered leaves. Halfway, though, my mother suddenly whirled about and I thought she had forgotten something important and she was to retrieve it but she did not run back to the building. I saw her whirl around and, for a while, I could not see her head because she had bowed so low and my father shielded her and patted her waist. *Cristo*, I thought I heard her say because she always said that when she got carried away. Go, I commanded Chito, help Papa bring her here. Go, Carmita seconded and it did not take long before they were back and my mother hugged her bag and the driver held her *anahaw* fan and my father was very pale. I heard the car door click, *Cristo*, it sounded like a sob.

Afterwards, of course, it would never be the same for the rest of us again. My father's car pulled up in the early evening and we heard his steps hurry past the pathway but he always forgot to hold the knob gently because the door banged whenever he came in. Papa, I would call and he would look up from his coffee and I would affect a startled face because he would still be in his socks, was he going out again? But who cared much for accidentals? That season, I threw away my old ribbons and burned the love letter whose grammatical errors I had corrected, but when I kissed my father's forehead in the early evening, I did not volunteer the information because he was too engrossed with his coffee and, besides, it seemed he never played his favorite fugue so that when I pushed the door, I heard only the buzzing of the air-conditioning unit, and the after-shave lotion did not smell as fresh and as neat any more because my father did not care to write to anyone and when he came home, he was red with summer's fever and we greeted each other in the pathway because I was leaving for my classes. I peered through the blinds when it was getting late and adjusted my curlers and waited for Carmita to stop her piano-playing and come up to sell some benefit ticket or flaunt the first Liszt she was assigned to, but after the notes died down, I heard her come up the stairs, walk past my room, her slippers gently slapping against the floor, and then I heard a door slam and I decided she was very tired. Supper was served hot at seven, like old times and Carmita and I talked about the neighbor's poodle and the classmate's complexion and my mother reprimanded Chito for letting his spoon hit the bowl's sides but it was never the same again because my father did not mutter *impossible* when the phone rang or the door bell sounded.

It was not easy to pluck eyebrows when it was very warm and a brother quietly sat on the bed's edge and cringed his nose. I had to shampoo my hair more often and dry my nylons a countless times because the days stretched and one was left with too much sweat and a deep longing for December. In the mornings, I leaned out of the window and saw the sprinkler on and I leaned out more to catch the smell of grass. The bougainvilleas were a riotous vermilion and they grew thick so that the stone wall that sliced my father's home apart from the rest of Artiaga did not suffer the season's length. My father's sister sent an orange butterfly chair and I claimed it and took it out to the year-torn verandah where I played solitaire until it was dark and the boys stopped biking up and down the lanes. When I got tired, I stretched my legs and learned how to smoke and dreamed of the things I would do after college. Oh, it was easy to think of the things you wanted for your life. When I was in grade school, we had a little song and a little game where we bent and stretched and reached for the sky and stood a-tiptoe and, everytime, the green-eyed madame made us catch something. I remember somebody catching a telephone and my seatmate grasping a pink giant and somebody else holding out an airplane and I was so embarrassed the first time because I could not think of anything so I just said, looking at her eyes, I got a green kite, Sister. She laughed and tugged at my pigtail and asked if my mother was teaching me the poems she taught in class for she was teaching then but I only clutched at my ribbon because it sounded weird. When I was six I dreamed I was a concert pianist. I marched into the living room and when my mother decided to show off, it was pleasant to have a daughter who could play some little waltz, *sigue, hija,* she would point to the piano and it was like a ritual, but one day I looked into the mirror long enough and decided I had thick eyebrows and they needed revision so that when I went down for lunch, I told Mother to excuse me from the piano teacher because I was not feeling well. I placed the pill she me gave into an empty powder box and started with the left eyebrow but I thought of the heroes I had marked with asterisks in the few books I had read and when the quotation was so long, I got carried away and the blade hurt my skin. My father and I used to talk about it often: we sat in the porch and I watched him pamper his pipe and listened to the time when I would finish college and go to Madrid and write many stories. I heard him talk about the farm he bought in Taytay and the poultry he would keep when he retired from the service and my mother would be free from all the impossible themes that made her irritable with the maids. I looked out into the garden and through the screen watched the sprinkler while adjusting a bobby pin. It all sounded uncomplicated, my father leaving the government and my mother would be leaving the University and Chito becoming an engineer and Carmita teaching piano and Pepito being ours forever, I dreamed of having read all the good books and heard all the good records and received the best grades and when my friends and I joked about the boys reserved for us, I silently thought of my mythology and someone playing a nocturne and a clipped accent and an impeccable grammar.

That summer though, I never heard my mother claim she was once young and very pretty in college. I went to borrow a book once and I found her seated on the edge of Father's bed and she had theme papers all around her but she only held her red pencil and she yawned when I came in. My mother had dark eyes and she graduated with a *magna* and she taught Victorian literature and she spoke good English but when she talked of that summer, she would let the grief spill like powder over the slip covers, into the drawers of her desk, before the cupboards, over and over again, but the quaver would stay and she would never learn how to express it well. Summer was a long May and a lot of dances and we made countless trips to the thrift shop but Carmita and I often came home with nothing save a halfslip or a tiny blue vase. Sometimes, I stayed in the University library and wrote to the friends I had not seen for quite sometime.

It was not fun to dance with boys you did not like, to joke with girls you had just met, to swim in a pool in a suit you did not approve of. I came home late and stayed awake and secretly wished the phone would ring and it would be an old friend back from a long trip. Never mind what time it was. I expected something to happen, somebody to ring the door bell and many letters to come and anybody to die in the neighborhood because that would be something to talk about. It was not fair, I thought, and when the neighbor trapped me in the grocery store, before a pile of potato chips, to ask how our Pepito was, I shoved my dark glasses up and said we sent clean pajamas everytime and accommodations cost fifteen pesos a day and, no, he was all right, he did not sleep on the cement and eat from a tin plate, but how was her son, was there a red mark again? It was a raw deal. I decided. We got good grades in school and said our grace before starting with the soup and my brother was not a bum. Nobody deserved it: our little crimes were limited to banging the phone or laughing over love letters that were not meant for us to read or taking bus rides without any destination. When I sat in the porch I remembered the green-eyed madame and knew it was the time for one's hidden wheat. Summer was a grey May and visitors who did not come and I watched the acacia serve as trap to a lot of kites and I knew it was not right to cry when my mother stopped dead still from the flowers she was arranging. I was graduating from college and I had read Newman and I thought of a second spring and how there would be a happier season for all of us. When I smoothed my pillows or dried my nylons, I thought Pepito would one day be back with us and I would make fruitcake with him and he would tinker the high notes when I played my worn-out pieces and I would slap his fingers gently but he would only stick his tongue out or run to the kitchen to ask for a cookie.

It was a long wait. I quarreled with Alex down the lane and he declared he could not understand me and he asked what the matter was but I said there was nothing wrong, I was not sick, I was just bored and he said I was impossible, I was always hoping for much. But it was not true. I only attended a choir meeting and sang hymns and when I went down the loft, all I expected was someone to call me for a chat. Regina, I thought I heard once, but when I looked back I saw no one and I shivered. If falling in love with someone who could play the piano only by ear was too much, then he was right.

But he would one day learn, I thought, and he would not shudder, I decided, he would like me that much and he would accept anything to make me cook his supper. I loved Pepito despite the fact that I would have to spoon-feed him forever and I fed on the thought that Alex would love him too and everything would be all right for all of us. Last night, Alex started to tell me about a party he had attended; but I would be back in the pathway, before my father, and I would hear him ask, how about your life, Regina, and I understood what he meant: he could never bear the thought of his son eating in the basement because a stranger could not stand someone spilling his aqua over the piano bench and powder over the slip covers and perfume over his dresser. I will never get married, I declared, and my father laughed softly and it was the strangest laughter I would ever hear.

May was long and it stared at us and all we did was fan ourselves endlessly or say the heat was terrible or why was it like that? Docked under the shower, I thought it would have been better had I run off with some stinking campus poet and my father would be too mad to ask what he had that deserved me, or Chito could have figured in some brawl but it would be nothing really because it was all a case of mistaken identity and so no grudges were bred, or Carmita could have seen a movie with someone Mother did not like and Father caught her having pizza pie with him and so he threatened to cut all piano lessons but it would still be all right because she would promise not to do it again. But not Pepito. I used to buy chocolates on my way home from school and Mother paid a boy to bathe him and play with him and feed him and we thought that as long as we did not permit him to go beyond the gate of my father's house, he would be safe and the world would not hurt him. I watched him pile his alphabet blocks and saw again the dark eyes and the firm mouth and the fair arms and the chubby fingers, oh my brother would grow up to be fair and good-looking but would that suffice, he grinned widely and his teeth were white and always clean, please, was that my brother's worth, only that, was that his slice of sky? I lay awake in the early afternoons and waited for the sounds of his many games but of course I was just being sentimental. We erred somewhere, I thought. With those we loved we would be most vulnerable, we would admit, but I'm afraid, but I'm scared, and we would not worry about sanitation and lysol and worms when we thought of kisses. Perhaps I did not have to go to college to find out that superman did not exist. When Alex looked up because I had brushed his hand aside it was only a foolish pride that I had affected for having sat in literature classes and having made the dean's list. You are the romanticist, Alex used to be very proud of his being in medical school, and I asked, so what?

I knew that I would one day marry Alex and we would have our own place and we would have our own children but I thought it was not right to speak of that time too much because it was May and it was stifling and when Alex asked why I was always hurrying home, I said someone more important was waiting for me, someone I liked, who could play the piano very well but I did not laugh when he threw a cigarette out and said I was impossible. Visit him, my father's sister would urge, but on Sundays, I watched my father's car cough away and then I returned to the living room and played a funny song. Last night stopped being the college dance or a movie or a pizza pie, last night from then on was my brother Pepito and a tray of lilies and I felt like throwing up each time. I walked up the pathway and it always occurred that it was just like this, it was warm and when I got home, it was already late afternoon and my blouse was soggy with sweat and my feet felt cramped. It was warm even in the living room and one of the lamps was on. My mother was comfortable in a massive chair and she was brushing her hair when I kissed her forehead. Again, she called out and my sister resumed her *valse*.

I went to Jefferson and I got two books for the report I'm making, I told her and she nodded. There is a butter cake from Tita Emma, she said, I told Chito to leave a piece for you. Is he home already, I asked, and when she looked up, as if startled, I was taken aback because her face was tired and haggard from crying. Careful, she called out as my sister ran off, loyal to the four sharps and her notes were crisp and rounded and flawless and, brushing off a lock of hair, I remembered I had not touched the keys for a long time. I yawned and stretched and I heard my mother repeat, there is a butter cake from Tita Emma.

Distinctly, the tempo *giusto ma brioso* followed me to my room and I did not know how tired I was until I sang the notes and ran out of breath. It was warm. Presently, I heard Chito suddenly say something and I found him seated on my bed's edge, so, embarrassed, I proceeded to the bathroom to take off my garter belt.

My slippers, please, I called out and they came flying and one even hit my left leg. I took off my blouse and wrapped the garter belt and threw the bundle back to the room. I heard the faint clicking of buttons.

You were out the whole day, Chito's voice seeped clearly through the splashing of water and I hurriedly washed off the soap from my hands.

I went to Jefferson, I found myself repeating. I'm making a report next week.

The whole day? His question made the toothpaste hurt my tongue.

You mean, I asked, you missed class? Are you sick, Chito?

He was still seated on the edge of my bed when I returned to the room. He cupped his chin and I was buttoning my blouse when I heard him say he had been waiting for me. The blouse lay limp on the floor and the garter belt actually hugged his toe.

Where have you been, he finally asked.

I did not approve of his tone. He was only nineteen and that made him a year younger and I thought it was not right to allow him to sound authoritative where the life of an older sister was concerned. You heard me, I snapped, bending to retrieve my things.

In the room, Carmita's *poco retinuto* was well-defined and I hooked a foot stool and yawned.

He straightened his back and rubbed his eyes with the back of his right palm. He looked sorry. But what's the matter with you again, I asked impatiently. Are you not feeling well?

He looked sick against the bright yellow of the lamplight. I moved the feet stool closer and touched his knee.

My brother and I were friends. On my birthday, he gave me an album of Chopin's waltzes and wrote, firmly and clearly, you might learn them yet, *señora*, your playing makes him weep but still you are my sister and everytime he stamps his feet, I also feel like throwing up. I embroidered a handkerchief for him in turn and slashed my allowance so he could be smart and happy at their college fair and when his friends dropped in on Saturday afternoons to talk about the girls whom they suspected loved them secretly, I was always good for a pitcher of orange juice and a tray of cold sandwiches. In my room Chito loafed about and used my writing desk and wasted my stationery for his love letters and when I shooed him away while I quarreled with my curlers, he paused still and browsed over my books before finally leaving. I skirted into his room and picked his blades for sharpening my pencils and, once, I needed a coin for some circle I was drawing and because I could not find any, I took the cover of his after-shave lotion but I was in such a great hurry that I toppled the bottle down and the aquamarine licked his dresser like an elongated tongue. Stop stealing my blades, he would storm into my room. It must have been Mama, I would dismiss him with a wave, laughter mixing with warm tea as I washed off the last trace of powder from my chin, she needed to sharpen her eyebrow pencil. You do not buy my aqua, he would glare, and I would clutch the towel and exclaim, *Que horror*, a miserable drop of aqua is nothing compared to ten beautiful sheets of stationery! *Impossible*, he would sneer and bang the door but he never meant it, I think, because very soon he would again be sneaking into my room to "borrow" the records he enjoyed lending to Ma. Paz, his girl from music school. For all his protests against my course and my pale blue nail polish and my college sweetheart, I missed a bowling session and made *pastillas* on his birthday. I still thought that Ma. Paz should be his alone, that he should one day top the board exams and be a better engineer than Father, that he did not deserve the friends who wore tight pants and bought nothing but Valentine cards and chewing gum and when he yawned and rubbed his eyes, I asked, did she throw a vase at you this time?

He stretched his arms and shook his head.

Chito, I cleared my throat, it is not right to answer back. He would be forever thinking that there was something wrong somewhere, I thought. He would always think that it was wrong to be reminded that drinking and gambling were vices when all he did was pester our party line, that it was stupid to be told this when he was already nineteen, in college and even taller than my father. He would be consistently considering it cramping, waging wars, but his were greater, he argued once, after all, what did I fight for, come, tell him, what was an eyebrow pencil and a lipstick tube and silly love letters? Chito, I slapped his arms, stop acting, you are too old for tantrums.

But we did not quarrel, he said.

Then why did you miss class?

He slapped a slipper against the floor. He looked up, as if startled. How could I go? He sounded tired and irritated.

I straightened my back and rubbed my knees. No, I thought, it could be Pepito. My youngest brother was feverish the whole week and he refused to eat his meals and he sat in the living room and stared at us.

Father had to come home, he said. Mother was hysterical.

I stood up and felt very tired. But what happened, I impatiently asked. It had to be something great and significant to all of us, either someone died or there was an accident: my mother never screamed or threw a vase, breeding was her favorite word and she loved to praise the boys who were civilized, who were clean, who were proper. I remember having sewn beads into my evening jacket and having declared I was madly in love but my mother did not look startled, she shrugged her shoulders and said, go, as long as he was all right and I stayed proper. It sounded good and kind until I fell in love with Alex and I realized what Mother meant that my sweetheart should be a *summa cum laude* and he should read poetry and he should be able to interpret *Prelude in A* and he should own a rosary. When I brush my hair, I wondered, God, where would I ever bump into him?

I saw her, I repeated.

She cried and cried, Chito recalled, and I heard Father say he has to be taken somewhere. He is not all right, Ate Regina, and I knew it was something bad because my brother seldom addressed me with such courtesy.

No, I said. I walked to the window and looked out but I saw nobody except a neighbor's son who was pedalling home in his blue bicycle. My brother was never all right, I thought. Mother made him blow the eight candles on his birthday cake. When he turned twelve he either nodded or shook his head and he never learned to make a wish. We thought of sending him to the new school on Sta. Mesa where they trained such children, never mind the expenses, I heard my father say, Pepito should have friends and learn how to write his name with them. I went there for a while but he eventually got tired of the attempt and would not get into the car when it was time for his classes and Mother said, never mind, let the child play with his ball in the garden and I assured my father that I would teach the child when I had the time to read and to write and I would tell him stories, but my father started the car and he did not come home for lunch that day.

He broke the plate and threw away his lunch, Chito said. He ran and spilled Mama's perfume over her bed and he would not stop until she hit him with a slipper. Papa called him but he hid behind the hedges and would not let anyone touch him.

It sounded pale. You should have been here, Chito said, but I felt very tired. I went to Jefferson, all right, but that was in the morning right after my classes. I saw Alex and we had lunch together and he accompanied me to buy a book and because the day was very warm and long, we went to see a movie. I did not care to understand what it was all about, the hero and the heroine touched too much but their kisses lacked meaning, they came too often and took so long and before they decided they could be together forever, I was busy trying to recall a dream I had the night before.

My brother and I were very quiet for a long time after that and when he spoke again, he wanted to know if it was true that such things could be inherited, was it that bad?

Quiet, I snapped and I was suddenly angry. I'll go and see him, I said and left him slapping a slipper against the floor.

The piano playing had stopped and a record was telling a tale about boat-rides and bells being tolled and there was only a maid polishing the coffee table. I found a tray of lilies beside the pile of Chito's records and I knew it was from my father's sister because she always sent me one when she came back from Thailand. Give me that, I said, and proceeded to the porch and down the steps, paused briefly by the hedges when I found my father smoking in the garden and he asked where I was going with the tray of flowers. I'll show them to Pepito, I said.

All of us knew we did not deserve it. I stood in the pathway and I thought I heard Mother call we would have supper but I talked on and Father said Pepito was in the garage with the driver and would not return to the house. I'll show him this, I said and hurried down the pathway, onto the curb, past the bushes and Quinto met me at the door and he said, He's there, Miss.

I know, I said as he pushed the door.

He went running about, Quinto volunteered, He's panting. I nodded and motioned him to open the door wider.

He does not know anybody any more, the driver continued and I shushed him up because the door was now open and Pepito was staring at us.

My brother looked tired, all right, and he looked sharp with his mouth set firm and he was leaning against the wall and he had his hands dangling between his legs. He looked fairer and thinner and when I said I had something for him, he jerked and cocked his head.

Come, I said. He stopped a few steps before me and eyed the tray suspiciously. From Tita Emma, I said and he cocked his head again.

The rest of the lilies quivered in my hands and my lips felt very dry. Atop the bed, Pepito stood with the lily that he had snatched. Around and around and around the lily went: *look*, his voice was distant and strange and he did not sound twelve, *look*, he urged, and I watched my brother, his shirt soggy with sweat and his face flushed and his lips pale.

Go down, I commanded, but it was hardly audible and, if he heard it, he did not mind at all because he kept on making faces and sticking his tongue out as if we were playmates quarreling from our respective fences. He waved his lily, he bit its stalk, he kissed its whiteness. Go down, I said, I repeated.

He looked up, startled, and I said, Ate Nang does not give that, Pepito. Ate Nang does not like bad boys.

His eyes appeared wild and deep-set and very dark. No, I thought, there was a time when he was all right. He ran about my father's house and tugged at Chito's kite. There was a time when my grandmother was alive and she looked out the window and said, *guapo*, that *nieto* would marry Miss Philippines. Did he fall from the sofa, from the piano bench, from the bed? But all babies fall, I heard my father drank and my mother said, never mind, never mind, Greg, we will get over this. My parents had both gone to college, they scolded us when we talked ill about the piano teacher and did not study our arithmetic, my parents heard Mass but they had no patience for stupidity. Pepito was God's gift to us, the father confessor loved to intone, and when the child came up to us and cocked his head or cringed his nose, we kissed his knuckles and rationalized, it was all right, the mind was not all that mattered, you could have an IQ of 145 but you were nothing if you did not know how to cry. We nestled the medals we got in school in dark-blue cushions and memorized our report cards but Pepito was the arm that linked us to the friends who received red marks or got shouted at: and when the car breezed past her terrace, we waved back at a neighbor who still had her curlers on.

But that should not have happened. He clutched the lily to his breast and shook his head, no, no, he stuck his tongue out and sank on his knees. He buried his face in the pile of pillows and kept on shaking his head.

Pepito, I called out and the name hurt my throat. Pepito, I pleaded and when he would not look up again, I let go of the tray of lilies and asked, feverish and quivering, what do you like, but what do you like?

None, none, he shook vigorously with protest. I held him by the shoulders and felt him sobbing. Chocolates, I smoothed his shirt, fruitcake? marshmallows?

He looked up at this and his face was flushed and his cheeks were wet. Ate Nang will give it to you Pepito, I promised, tell Ate Nang what you want.

He knitted his brows and shivered and coughed. He stared at the ceiling, then he widened his eyes and closed them and shivered again and when he wound his arms about my waist, I felt him trembling. I stroked his nape and rumpled his hair and asked, what was it Pepito? Tell Ate Nang what you saw.

His arms tightened about my waist and he buried his face in my breast. He made a long eerie sound and shook his head again. Sssh, I patted his cheek and cupped his chin but when he would not stop, I buried my face in his head and all at once my nose caught my mother's perfume and I realized it had been a terrible afternoon. Pepito, I softly called and in the room the eerie sound was Carmita's *valse* and over the pile of pillows, there was Chito and he asked his question again and nobody shushed him because the room was pitch dark and it was very late. My father stood by a window, his grief silent and vast and deep but in my mind it was less terrible because he had his fists clenched and he was able to scream, *Por Dios.*

Mother was on the floor, she hugged his knees but she could not reach him, she did not say, never mind Greg, never mind, we shall get over this soon, because prostrate and dark on the floor, her grief built a wall between their faces and over the crisp rounded notes I heard her ask, why this, why this? Mama, her perfume hurt my nose and Pepito's tears trickled through my palm and when the tears blurred my sight at last, I remembered, this must have been last night's important dream, perhaps, I could not recall it but it was all right, here it was, blurred and tear-washed and killing and when the remainder sank down my throat, I felt it solid and deep and irrevocable like the reality that down the lanes Alex and I shall walk and laugh and talk about the garden we would keep and the meals we would share and the sons we shall have and the wind would dry off the sweat from our bodies but it would be fast Angelus and the cars would pull up and telephone calls would have to be promised because, *santisima*, it was late and there were suppers to have.✿

Cost Price

Kerima Polotan

WHEN THE cokes were finally set before them and Isabel had taken a sip and rested a little, her unhappiness began to lift. How easy it was for her to forget not why she had wept but that she had wept on this lovely afternoon as she sat behind some underbrush out on that forsaken park near the bay.

"Better?" Joe asked.

"Yes," she said quickly, "but don't talk to me, Joe. Not yet." She could not weep here, Isabel thought, looking around at the badly lighted eating place. If they talked of it, she would surely want to cry and how possibly could she in this crowd of pickpockets and stevedores and churchgoers, in this one more of the places to which Joe and she came after an afternoon on the seawall or the park, this dirty parlor with the sodden floors, the cockroaches and the obscenities on the walls?

Out in the park earlier that afternoon, there had not been too many people. Except for two other pairs who passed them unheeding, and themselves disappeared among the trees, the park had been empty, shrouded with that quality of open privacy which was both its gift and bane. It had not seemed shameless to part the brush and creep behind it, then kiss on the grass while they touched each other with warm, trembling hands. But the inevitable turn came. She pushed him away, sitting up, brushing her skirt and tucking her legs beneath her. With her face turned away, she said, "No. No." And as if those words were a signal, there were suddenly all the things they seldom spoke of, crowding them where they rested on the rise. Joe's sick parents. The difficult and futile night studies. The miserable jobs they both held. So the quarrel was born once more, and spent itself as it had done countless times before, with the terrible killing words and the tears of despair.

Where Isabel sat crying, she felt someone must surely hear her sobs and come to ask why she wept, and how was she to say that she wept because Joe desired her, but they were poor and could not marry? Time flies, love dies! Love dies! and she gestured Joe caught her hand and held it, saying gently, "It is such a lovely afternoon, Isabel."

Here in the half-dark, it was not too difficult to strangle desire and begin to talk calmly. She leaned back and listened to him, feeling her love shake off its bruises, shriven of the afternoon's physical urgency. "I might yet get that raise," he said.

Joe worked in a publishing house, copying out research notes on small white cards and filing them for someone more important to come and read and throw into disarray. "With that raise, we can go ahead," he said, leaning forward to draw a paper napkin. He bent over it and proceeded to make a neat row of figures. "Look, even with Father and Mother, it's possible. With that raise." Isabel picked up the paper. He had thrown such things across the table to her, in the possibly thousand afternoons they had met after that first time, napkins on which he figured rent and food and medicine and clothes, tossing them over to Isabel who clipped them together, the pink and the yellow and the white restaurant tissues, keeping them as she would keep this one, holding it like a receipt against today's tears.

Isabel's job was as assistant librarian to Mrs. Suntay, in a small children's reading room tucked away in a quiet street, rare in the heart of what was toughie-town. She doubled as clerk and sometimes even as janitor. The pay was small but there were compensations. The quonset hut that hugged the middle of the barren yard was like another home to her. Mrs. Suntay and she had fixed a corner, cutting it from view with a big bookcase and dragging a cot into it. At noon, she or the older woman took turns resting on it, or they sat together and chatted quietly. Mrs. Suntay's gentleness made the intimacy possible.

During Liberation, a first-aid unit run by Americans had been housed in the building. They had thoughtfully built into it a faucet and shower. The succeeding tenants of the place (a minor government bureau, a short-lived puericulture center, and this library) had not bothered to board up the room. Now, two galvanized sheets lined its walls. A cut of plastic cloth gave it added privacy. Isabel and Mrs. Suntay came with extra slips and on warm noons took refreshing baths before settling down to lunch. It was all in all a happy arrangement, but when payday rolled around and the boy from the Main walked up with their envelopes, the temptation to feel bitter was strong. Mrs. Suntay would count her pay, peeling the bills off one by one and laying them on her desk wordlessly, a naked look coming suddenly over her face. Isabel would turn away, hating to see the ritual, her own sweaty fingers closing nervously about the miserable wages. Then Mrs. Suntay would sigh, "Oh well, there's the bathroom." It was a simple joke but heart-lifting; it held them together. Isabel remembered it when she was sweeping beneath the low tables or when the truck disgorged milk boxes full of torn editions.

Sometimes when a supervisor was conscience-stricken, a note would arrive saying the projection unit was dropping by in the afternoon—there would be movies for the children. At the news, the kids would push their chairs away and go flying out of the door to spread the tidings through the choked alleys of the vicinity, and in the afternoon, a hundred of them sat awed through an hour of colored romping animals.

Once, they ran a particularly old copy that sputtered and died, rasping, halfway. The fragile magic tore and fell to pieces, leaving the children restless. Mrs. Suntay and Isabel sought out the man and pleaded but there was nothing he could do. "It's a beat-up thing," he said, wiping his forehead and looking around at the closed windows. They could feel the children waiting, and the man relented. "The driver can run back for another," he said, "if you can hold your audience here."

It was on this afternoon that Isabel first met Joe. He had slipped in quietly and stood waiting for the show to end. He had four books under his arm and crossed the room to her when the children were gone. "This is a children's library," she snapped impatiently, the rest of her angry reproof dying unsaid at the sight of his dusty shirt, a blob of several colors where the dye had run. "I came to sell books," he said. Mrs. Suntay explained they never bought books but waited instead for whatever the other branches threw their way. But seeing how his shoulders drooped, she suggested that he leave a book or two for a week, and if the children liked them, they would ask the office to buy them for the library.

Joe was profuse with his thanks as he retreated to the door and stumbled down the steps.

He was to tell her much later how he had been sent out that morning to try to sell copies of books that the owners had overstocked. None of their agents would touch them. The schools had sent their samples back. The owners had looked at all their employees and picked out five from those who were low-salaried and could not afford to displease. Jose had been one of those. He had left his precious cards behind, closing his encyclopedias and shutting off the light above his corner, beaten and bitter. He would feel even more God-awfully lonely later in the day when no one would look at the books, and doors were being shut in his face—house door, church door, shop door. No one wanted a book—not the housewife who peeped through a window and thought he had come to bludgeon her with Grimm's, or the priest who waved him aside and said he had several confessions to make, or the tailor with the tape wound about his neck who did not lift his head once, and when he was through, proceeded to measure Joe for a suit.

FROM THE BEGINNING, poverty was the unnamed specter. They spent their afternoons brightly on the seawall, feasting on boiled peanuts and talking. There was so much to talk about, for these two who had met each other at some fortunate turn in the many devious paths of the hot and crowded city. Isabel lived through those first days in a fever of wings and unending wonder. In Mrs. Suntay, who listened quietly to her confidences, she had a grave, interested audience. The older woman liked Joe and once even lightly offered him the use of the shower on an afternoon when he had limped into the room, almost prostrate from the heat.

They talked of marriage in the beginning in the breathless, gay manner of lovers trying to fool themselves, but the lightheartedness soon wore away and left them unhappy. All the new, exciting things to talk of were quickly exhausted.

They kissed and put their arms about each other and there were suddenly things in Isabel's mind, curled there like white worms, stirring slowly to life. Sometimes when hand slipped or his lips lingered, Isabel pulled away frightened, and there would be a fight, fierce but brief, for Joe was always asking to be forgiven.

One afternoon, she said, "Let's think, Joe." She knew he understood what she meant: let's stop and think now, Joe, we can't be riding buses forever. Where he sat beside her in the lumbering vehicle, Joe shifted uncomfortably. He had come for her, looking tired and lonely, and despite her quiet resolve to be gay, the words had leaped out before she could stop herself.

The rain that afternoon had bathed both sky and street and it seemed to Isabel as they got off that the very grass they walked on grew with hope beneath their feet. Joe chose his words carefully. There were things, Isabel knew about them. His sick parents and his small pay. The old man's cough. The mother's kidneys. He envied the effrontery of the other fellows who merely walked up to his boss, but if he did that he was more likely to talk himself out of his job. He asked, "Have you seen the house, Isabel?" she shook her head. He continued, "It's a room above an estero." She heard the rushing wings of the first twilight birds. She said, breathing deeply, "All right. You owe me nothing. This is enough," and opened her arms to include the quiet evening.

But saying goodbye at the gate to her dormitory that night, Joe held her back by the hand to ask, "Do you believe me, Isabel?"

"My dear clerk," she said tenderly. "Joe. Joe."

"Tell me. Do you believe what I am, Isabel?"

"Why?"

"Because I want you," he said simply.

Isabel looked at him; one foot on the landing: face lifted to her, Joe who had named desire at last and given to it the form of his body and the sound of his voice.

One day, he called up to ask if she might wish to go to a show? He had added that he had the money all right, a five-peso bill he had put away sometime ago against some such day as this when he might wish to buy a few hours of joy with her. Would she go? "Things will be all right," he said with a hint of laughter. He was probably holding the machine close to his mouth, his voice was loud and near, "I'm going to try and not be any trouble." Then more thoughtfully, "Do you hear me, Isabel? About last time, please forgive me. And yet I'm not all apology. I'm sorry only because it made you feel wrong."

She stood with her back to Mrs. Suntay. She held the phone quietly checking the sudden tears, remembering how he had flung his arms that time and said aloud to the empty dark about them. "You can kill a man this way, you know."

Now he went on, "Are you there, Isabel?"

"Yes."

"Will you go tonight?"

"Yes."

"Try to forget last time, won't you?"

"I will, Joe."

"Was I particularly ugly? But I suppose I was."

"I guess so."

"Next time, you get yourself a whistle and blow it. I'll stop."

"I'll remember that, Joe."

"Isabel—"

"Yes?"

"That still doesn't make it wrong, you know, or cheap. Out here," (star and hill and grass) "I loved you very much. It seemed the most natural wish and I couldn't see where anyone had anything to do with it, where the world came into it at all—"

"We won't talk of it, or think about it anymore."

"...And you were wrong. I don't go around wanting to raise as many skirts as I can. Sure it was sex, but it was also love, and all the good things that go with it."

Inside the cool theater, they did not talk of it again. They sat instead, watching the beautiful men and women move on the screen, speaking the careful, meaninged words, contorting their faces into grimaces of pain and joy and falling upon each other in embraces that seemed to resolve everything.

Here, leaning against a cushioned seat, holding hands with Joe, it was possible to hope again. One's dreams did not die. The movies lifted you without effort from a world of ten-cent dates and soggy eating places into another of color and music and fortunate circumstance where romance bloomed happily in upholstered bedrooms. Isabel watched her own heart's dreams live briefly on a white screen, saw herself enclosed in a lasting embrace beyond the reach of fear.

She bit into the heel of her palm, fighting the growing misery, fighting the tears. Joe's arms were around her, drawing her face close to his shirt, his mouth against her ears. "Isabel, Isabel," he said, speaking her name in a voice faint with love. She began to cry at last. Huddled in the leather chair, in the dark that was like all the nights they had wanted for their own, Isabel began to weep.

Joe held her tightly at first, then loosely, helplessly. He patted her shoulder and said. "I'm sorry."

Spoken against the rising music and the ripple of candy foil about them, Joe's words seemed to Isabel the final defeat. Still held in his arms, she lifted her face to his own warm and living one, moist against the shadows, and said the words at last, "Joe, when Mrs. Suntay leaves. I have the key."

THE UNLIGHTED reading room looked larger than it really was even when Isabel closed the door upon the street outside. In the tiny space behind the bookcase, they stood silently for a few moments, two shadows among the many others in the room. There was suddenly nothing to say. Nothing, nothing, Isabel thought, here where they finally stood, beside the obtruding cot about which they had argued a million times and on whose countless fears she had crucified herself again and again.

They stumbled toward each other at the same time and began to kiss, lightly at first, as though not sure they might do so without fear of discovery in the room, and then deeply. His lips were over her face all at once, his fingers tracing a tender pattern on eye and cheek. "Isabel," he said brokenly. "Take me. On faith."

She kissed him and then tried to move away from him a little but he would not let her go. She stepped blindly back and fell against the edge of the cot, then athwart it, and she had a picture of how she must look, sprawled awkwardly, skirt away, legs kicking. She saw him clearly standing above her and shut her eyes against him, certain that the cheap thin shirt that had come unbuttoned was threadbare at the collar. She held him off with one hand, while her mind ran mercilessly on—and his shoes were scuffed; his socks, unmended; his handkerchief, old; his pockets, empty.

When Joe bent once more to lift her, she brushed his hands aside. He looked at her uncomprehendingly and approached again. She was suddenly, inexplicably angry. She stood up quickly and in one unreasoned crazy moment, swung at him and hit his face. Joe put his arms about her but Isabel was stronger than he expected and she raised her fists and swung senseless blows upon him, hitting his face and chest, striking him for all the many hills of previous dusks that she had wept upon.

Joe caught her hands and pushed her away.

"We need some air," he said tonelessly, unlocking a window.

"Turn on the light!"

"Of course," Joe said, and he was far away.

"Turn on the light!"

Joe gestured wearily, "I don't want to fight Isabel. There's no need. We've killed everything."

He stood in a corner, pushed beyond the reach of moonlight streaming in through the window. As strangely as it had come, her anger left her and only the tautnesss of remembered desire remained. Afterwards, that too (the soft, the sweet confusion) receded, fled.

"We shouldn't have gone to that movie. All those weeping violins," Joe said.

Tearless and still, Isabel stood there knowing that in a little while he was going to leave her and she would be alone to search for the anguished pieces of their selves that lay shattered about the tiny room. ✿

The Small Key

Paz Latorena

I

IT WAS very warm. The sun, up above a sky that was all blue and tremendous and beckoning to birds ever on the wing, shone bright as if determined to scorch everything under heaven, even the low, square nipa house that stood in unashamed relief against the gray green haze of grass and leaves.

It was a lonely dwelling, located far from its neighbors, which were huddled close to one another as if for mutual comfort. It was flanked on both sides by tall, slender bamboo trees which rustled plaintively under a gentle wind.

On the porch a woman past her early twenties stood regarding the scene before her with eyes made incurious by its familiarity. All around her the land stretched endlessly, it seemed, and vanished into the distance. There were dark, newly plowed furrows where in due time timorous seedlings would give rise to sturdy stalks and golden grain, to a rippling yellow sea in the wind and sun during harvest time. Promise of plenty and reward for hard toil! With a sigh of discontent, however, the woman turned and entered a small dining room where a man sat over a belated midday meal.

Pedro Buhay, a prosperous farmer, looked up from his plate and smiled at his wife as she stood framed by the doorway, the sunlight glinting on her dark hair, which was drawn back, without a relenting wave, from a rather prominent and austere brow.

"Where are the shirts I ironed yesterday?" she asked as she approached the table.

"In my trunk, I think," he answered.

"Some of them need darning," and, observing the empty plate, she added, "do you want some more rice?"

"No," hastily, "I am in a hurry to get back. We must finish plowing the south field today because tomorrow is Sunday."

Pedro pushed the chair back and stood up. Soledad began to pile the dirty dishes one on top of the other.

"Here is the key to my trunk." From the pocket of his khaki coat he pulled a string of nondescript red, which held together a big shiny key and another small, rather rusty-looking one.

With deliberate care, he untied the knot and, detaching the big key, dropped the small one back into his pocket. She watched him fixedly as he did this. The smile left her face and a big strange look came into her eyes as she took the big key from him without a word. Together they left the dining room.

Out on the porch, he put an arm around her shoulders and peered into her shadowed face.

"You look pale and tired," he remarked softly. "What have you been doing all morning?"

"Nothing," she said listlessly, "but the heat gives me a headache."

"Then lie down and try to sleep while I am gone." For a moment they looked deep into each other's eyes.

"It is really warm," he continued. "I think I will take off my coat."

He removed the garment absent-mindedly and handed it to her. The stairs creaked under his weight as he went down.

"Choleng," he turned his head as he opened the gate, "I shall pass by Tia Maria's house and tell her to come. I may not return before dark."

Soledad nodded. Her eyes followed her husband down the road, noting the fine set of his head and shoulders, the ease of his stride. A strange ache rose in her throat.

She looked at the coat as he handed it to her. It exuded a faint smell of his favorite cigars, one of which he invariably smoked, after the day's work, on his way home from the fields. Mechanically, she began to fold the garment.

As she was doing so, a small object fell to the floor with a dull, metallic sound. Soledad stopped down and picked it up. It was the small key! She stared at it in her palm as if she had never seen it before. Her mouth was tightly drawn and for a while she looked almost old.

She passed into the small bedroom and tossed the coat carelessly on the back of a chair. She opened the window and the early afternoon sunshine flooded in. On a mat spread on the bamboo floor were some newly washed garments.

She began to fold them one by one in a feverish haste, as if seeking in the task of the moment a refuge from painful thoughts. But her eyes moved restlessly around the room until they rested almost furtively on a small trunk that was half-concealed by a rolled mat in a dark corner.

It was a small, old trunk, without anything on the outside that might arouse one's curiosity. But it held the things she had come to hate with unreasoning violence, the things that were causing her so much unnecessary anguish and pain, and threatened to destroy all that was most beautiful between her and her husband!

Soledad came across a torn garment. She threaded a needle, but after a few uneven stitches she pricked her fingers and a crimson drop stained the white garment. Then she saw she had been mending on the wrong side.

"What is the matter with me?" she asked herself aloud as she pulled the thread with nervous and impatient fingers.

What did it matter if her husband chose to keep the clothes of his first wife?

"She is dead, anyhow. She is dead," she repeated to herself over and over again.

The sound of her own voice calmed her. She tried to thread the needle once more. But she could not, for the tears had come unbidden and completely blinded her.

"My God!" she cried with a sob, "make me forget Indo's face as he put the small key back into his pocket."

She brushed her tears with the sleeve of her camisa and abruptly stood up. The heat was stifling, and the silence in the house was beginning to be unendurable.

She looked out of the window. She wondered what was keeping Tía María. Perhaps Pedro had forgotten to pass by her house in his hurry. She could picture him out there in the south field gazing far and wide at the newly plowed land, with no thought in his mind but of work, work. For, to the people of the barrio whose patron saint, San Isidro Labrador, smiled on them with benign eyes from his crude altar in the little chapel up the hill, this season was a prolonged hour of passion during which they were blind and deaf to everything but the demands of the land.

During the next half hour, Soledad wandered in and out of the rooms, in an effort to seek escape from her own thoughts and to fight down an overpowering impulse. If Tía María would only come and talk to her to divert her thoughts to other channels!

But the expression on her husband's face as he put the small key back into his pocket kept torturing her like a nightmare, goading her beyond endurance. Then, with all resistance to the impulse gone, she was kneeling before the small trunk. There was an unpleasant, metallic sound for the key had not been used for a long time and it was rusty.

II

THAT EVENING Pedro Buhay hurried home with the usual cigar dangling from his mouth, pleased with himself and the tenants because the work in the south field had been finished. He was met by Tía María at the gate and was told by her that Soledad was in bed with a fever.

"I shall go to town and bring Doctor Santos," he decided, his cool hand on his wife's brow.

Soledad opened her eyes.

"Don't, Indo," she begged with a vague terror in her eyes which he took for anxiety for him because the town was pretty far and the road was dark and deserted by that hour of the night. "I shall be all right tomorrow."

Pedro returned an hour later, very tired and rather worried. The doctor was not at home but his wife had promised to give him Pedro's message as soon as he came in.

Tía María decided to remain for the night. But it was Pedro who stayed up to watch the sick woman. He was puzzled and worried—more than he cared to admit. It was true that Soledad had not looked very well early that afternoon. Yet, he thought, the fever was rather sudden. He was afraid it might be a symptom of a serious illness.

Soledad was restless the whole night. She tossed from one side to another, but towards morning she fell into some sort of troubled sleep. Pedro then lay down to snatch a few winks.

He woke up to find the soft morning sunshine streaming through the half-open window. He got up without making any noise. His wife was still asleep and now breathing evenly. A sudden rush of tenderness came over him at sight of her—so slight, so frail.

Tía María was nowhere to be seen, but that did not bother him for it was Sunday and the work in the south field was finished. However, he missed the pleasant aroma which came from the kitchen every time he work up early in the morning.

The kitchen looked neat but cheerless, and an immediate search for wood brought no results. So, shouldering an ax, Pedro descended the rickety stairs that led to the backyard.

The morning was clear and the breeze soft and cool. Pedro took in a deep breath of air. It was good—it smelt of trees, of the rice fields, of the land he loved.

He found a pile of logs under the young mango tree near the house, and began to chop. He swung the ax with rapid clean sweeps, enjoying the feel of the smooth wooden handle in his palms.

As he stopped for a while to mop his brow, his eye caught the remnants of a smudge that had been built in the backyard.

"Ah!" he muttered to himself. "She swept the yard yesterday after I left her. That, coupled with the heat, must have given her a headache and then the fever."

The morning breeze stirred the ashes and a piece of white cloth fluttered into view.

Pedro dropped his ax. It was a half-burnt *pañuelo*. Somebody had been burning clothes. He examined the slightly ruined garment closely. A doubting and puzzled expression came into his eyes. First, it was doubt groping for truth, then amazement, and finally agonized incredulity passed across his face. He almost ran back to the house. In three strides he was upstairs. He found his coat hanging from the back of a chair.

Cautiously he entered the room. The heavy breathing of his wife told him that she was still asleep. As he stood by the small trunk, a vague distaste to open it assailed him. Surely, he must be mistaken. She could not have done it. She could not have been that...that foolish.

Resolutely he opened the trunk. It was empty.

It was nearly noon when the doctor arrived. He felt Soledad's pulse and asked questions which she answered in monosyllables. Pedro stood by listening to the whole procedure with an inscrutable expression on his face. He had the same expression when the doctor told him that nothing was really wrong with his wife although she seemed to be worried about something. The physician merely prescribed a day of complete rest.

Pedro lingered on the porch after the doctor had left. He was trying not to be angry with his wife. He hoped it would be just an interlude that could be recalled without bitterness. She would explain sooner or later, she would be repentant, perhaps she would even try to convince him that she had done it because she loved him. And he would listen and eventually forgive her for she was young and he loved her. But somehow he knew that this incident would always remain a shadow in their lives.

How quiet and peaceful the day was! A cow that had strayed by looked over her shoulder with a round vague inquiry and went on chewing her cud, blissfully unaware of such things as a gnawing fear in the heart of a woman and a still smouldering resentment in a man's. ✿

Love in the Cornhusks

Aida Rivera-Ford

TINANG STOPPED before the Señora's gate and adjusted the baby's cap. The dogs that came to bark at the gate were strange dogs, big-mouthed animals with a sense of superiority. They stuck their heads through the hogfence, lolling their tongues and straining. Suddenly, from the gumamela row, a little black mongrel emerged and slithered through the fence with ease. It came to her, head down and body quivering.

"Bantay, Ay, Bantay!" she exclaimed as the little dog laid its paws upon her skirt to sniff the baby on her arm. The baby was afraid and cried. The big animals barked with displeasure.

Tito, the younger master, had seen her and was calling to his mother. "Ma, it's Tinang. Ma, Ma, it's Tinang." He came running down to open the gate.

"Aba, you are so tall now, Tito."

She smiled her girl's smile as he stood by, warding the dogs off. Tinang passed quickly up the veranda stairs lined with ferns and many-colored bougainvillea. On the landing, she paused to wipe her shoes carefully. About her, the Señora's white and lavender butterfly orchids fluttered delicately in the sunshine. She noticed though that the purple waling-waling that had once been her task to shade from the hot sun with banana leaves and to water with a mixture of charcoal and eggs and water was not in bloom.

"Is no one covering the waling-waling now?" Tinang asked. "It will die."

"Oh, the maid will come to cover the orchids later."

The Señora called from inside. "Ano, Tinang, let me see your baby. Is it a boy?"

"Yes, Ma," Tito shouted from downstairs. "And the ears are huge!"

"What do you expect?" replied his mother. "His father is a Bagobo. Even Tinang looks like a Bagobo now."

Tinang laughed and felt a warmness for her former mistress and the boy Tito. She sat self-consciously on the black narra sofa, for the first time a visitor. Her eyes clouded. The sight of the Señora's flaccidly plump figure, swathed in a loose waistless housedress that came down to her ankles, and the faint scent of *agua de colonia* blended with kitchen spice, seemed to her the essence of the comfortable world, and she sighed thinking of the long walk home through the mud, the baby's legs straddled to her waist, and Inggo, her husband, waiting for her, his body stinking of *tuba* and sweat, squatting on the floor, clad only in his foul undergarments.

"Ano, Tinang, is it not a good thing to be married?" the Señora asked, pitying Tinang because her dress gave way at the placket and pressed at her swollen breasts. It was, as a matter of fact, a dress she had given Tinang a long time ago.

"It is hard, Señora, very hard. Better that I were working here again."

"There!" the Señora said. "Didn't I tell you what it would be like, huh?...that you would be a slave to your husband and that you would work with a baby eternally strapped to you. Are you not pregnant again?"

Tinang squirmed at the Senora's directness but admitted she was.

"Hala! You will have a dozen before long." The Señora got up. "Come, I will give you some dresses and an old blanket that you can cut into things for the baby."

They went into a cluttered room which looked like a huge closet and as the Señora sorted out some clothing Tinang asked, "How is Señor?"

"Ay, he is always losing his temper over the tractor drivers. It is not the way it was when Amado was here. You remember what a good driver he was. The tractors were always kept in working condition. But now... I wonder why he left all of a sudden. He said he would be gone for only two days."

"I don't know," Tinang said. The baby began to cry. Tinang hushed him with irritation.

"Oy, Tinang, come to the kitchen; your Bagobito is hungry."

For the next hour, Tinang sat in the kitchen with an odd feeling; she watched the girl who was now in possession of the kitchen work around with a handkerchief clutched in one hand. She had lipstick on, too, Tinang noted. The girl looked at her briefly but did not smile. She set down a can of evaporated milk for the baby and served her coffee and cake. The Señora drank coffee with her and lectured about keeping the baby's stomach bound and training it to stay by itself so she could work. Finally, Tinang brought up, haltingly, with phrases like "if it will not offend you" and "if you are not too busy," the purpose of her visit—which was to ask Señora to be a *madrina* in baptism. The Señora readily assented and said she would provide the baptismal clothes and the fee for the priest. It was time to go.

"When are you coming again, Tinang?" the Señora asked as Tinang got the baby ready. "Don't forget the bundle of clothes and... oh, Tinang, you better stop by the drugstore. They asked me once whether you were still with us. You have a letter there and I was going to open it to see if there was bad news but I thought you would be coming."

A letter! Tinang's heart beat violently. Somebody is dead; I know somebody is dead, she thought. She crossed herself and after thanking the Señora profusely, she hurried down. The dogs came forward and Tito had to restrain them. "Bring me some young corn next time, Tinang," he called after her.

Tinang waited a while at the drugstore which was also the post office of the barrio. Finally, the man turned to her: "Mrs., do you want medicine for your baby or for yourself?"

"No, I came for my letter. I was told I have a letter."

"And what is your name, Mrs.?" he drawled.

"Constantina Tirol."

The man pulled a box and slowly went through the pile of envelopes most of which were scribbled in pencil. "Tirol, Tirol, Tirol..." He finally pulled out a letter and handed it to her. She stared at the unfamiliar scrawl. It was not from her sister and she could think of no one else who would write to her.

Santa Maria, she thought; maybe something has happened to my sister.

"Do you want me to read it for you?"

"No, no." She hurried from the drugstore, crushed that he should think her illiterate. With the baby on one arm and the bundle of clothes on the other and the letter clutched in her hand, she found herself walking toward home.

The rains had made a deep slough of the clay road and Tinang followed the prints left by the men and the carabaos that had gone before her to keep from sinking in mud up to her knees. She was deep in the road before she became conscious of her shoes. In horror, she saw that they were coated with thick, black clay. Gingerly, she pulled off one shoe after the other with the hand still clutching the letter. When she had tied the shoes together with the laces and had slung them on an arm, the baby, the bundle, and the letter were all smeared with mud.

There must be a place to put the baby down, she thought, desperate now about the letter. She walked on until she spotted a corner of a field where cornhusks were scattered under a kalamansi tree. She shoved together piles of husks with her foot and laid the baby down upon it. With a sigh, she drew the letter from the envelope. She stared at the letter which was written in English.

My dearest Tinay,

Hello, how is life getting along? Are you still in good condition? As for myself, the same as usual. But you're far from my side. It is not easy to be far from our lover.

Tinay, do you still love me? I hope your kind and generous heart will never fade. Someday or somehow I'll be there again to fulfill our promise.

Many weeks and months have elapsed. Still I remember our bygone days. Especially when I was suffering with the heat of the tractor under the heat of the sun. I was always in despair until I imagine your personal appearance coming forward bearing the sweetest smile that enabled me to view the distant horizon.

Tinay, I could not return because I found that my mother was very ill. That is why I was not able to take you as a partner of life. Please respond to my missive at once so that I know whether you still love me or not. I hope you did not love anybody except myself.

I think I am going beyond the limit of your leisure hour so I close with best wishes to you, my friends Gonding, Serafin, Bondio, etc.

Yours forever,

Amado

P.S. My mother died last month.

Address your letter: Mr. Amado Galuran
Binalunan, Cotabato

It was Tinang's first love letter. A flush spread over her face and crept into her body. She read the letter again. "It is not easy to be far away from our lover... I imagine your personal appearance coming forward... Someday, somehow I'll be there to fulfill our promise..." Tinang was intoxicated. She pressed herself against the kalamansi tree.

My lover is true to me. He never meant to desert me. Amado, she thought. Amado.

PACKING LIST

LAPENA=12 PHILIPPINE WOMEN WRITERS   1

University of Hawai'i Press
2840 KOLOWALU STREET
HONOLULU, HAWAI'I 96822-1888

WAREHOUSE CODE	PACKED BY	DATE	NO. CTN.	INVOICE NO.
				917929

And she cried, remembering the young girl she was less than two years ago when she would take food to the Señor in the field and the laborers would eye her furtively. She thought herself above them for she was always neat and clean and in her hometown, before she went away to work, she had gone to school and had reached the sixth grade. Her skin, too, was not as dark as those of the girls who worked in the fields weeding around the clumps of abaca. Her lower lip jutted out disdainfully when the farm hands spoke to her with many flattering words. She laughed when a Bagobo with two hectares of land asked her to marry him. It was only Amado, the tractor driver, who could look at her and make her lower her eyes. He was very dark and wore filthy and torn clothes on the farm, but on Saturdays when he came up to the house for his week's salary, his hair was slicked down and he would be dressed as well as Mr. Jacinto, the school-teacher. Once he told her that he would study in the city night-schools and take up mechanical engineering someday. He had not said much more to her, but one afternoon when she was bidden to take some bolts and tools to him in the field, a great excitement came over her. The shadows moved fitfully in the bamboo groves she passed and the cool November air edged into her nostrils sharply. He stood unmoving beside the tractor with tools and parts scattered on the ground around him. His eyes were a black glow as he watched her draw near. When she held out the bolts, he seized her wrist and said, "Come," pulling her to the screen of trees beyond. She resisted but his arms were strong. He embraced her roughly and awkwardly, and she trembled and gasped and clung to him...

A little green snake slithered languidly into the tall grass a few yards from the *kalamansi* tree. Tinang started violently and remembered her child. It lay motionless on the mat of husk. With a shriek she grabbed it wildly and hugged it close. The baby awoke from its sleep and cried lustily. *Ave Maria Santisima.* Do not punish me, she prayed, searching the baby's skin for marks. Among the cornhusks, the letter fell unnoticed. ✿

The Lot

Albina P. Fernandez

THE SPADE bit into the earth with a sharp, crisp crunch. When it was pulled out a fat earthworm came up with it, split into two but still squirming. Mrs. Razon watched the creature until it moved no more. Picking half of it with a twig, she examined the bits of soil clinging to it, more than ever convinced of the fertility of this patch of earth. Already, she could visualize shrubs profuse with flowers, perhaps violets, reminding one and all that the land they beautifully enclosed was privately owned. From crust to bottom, as far as the earth's core, it was hers, hers, hers!

"Drink your coffee, my dear. I bet you a kiss you did not catch a single word of my exegesis on Leibnitz's monadology," Mr. Razon said, as he held out his arms to gather his wife in an embrace. "Land prospecting again, are we?" he amiably asked, then paused as he noted the look Mrs. Razon gave him, a look starting from his greying head, slithering down like a snake along his slim frame, and down to his feet, then her eyes went up again and stopped at his neck, as though to encircle it. It was enough to make him stop short, even as he gurgled an unintelligible sound, as though his lecturer's voice had suddenly gone.

Mrs. Razon once more watched the fade-out of her recurrent dream, like a film cut short. But she would run it again, that picture of a piece of real estate, although next time the location and size might be different. Sometimes, when she could really bring herself to believe that Mr. Razon would one day earn princely royalties from his books, "the distinct Filipino contribution to philosophy" as he put it, his very own words, the lot would be large, located in a first-class subdivision. Other times, it was a small lot in some government low-cost housing project. Now, with the sudden bursting of her latest visualization, that hedge, those violets, she became exceedingly vexed, "Indeed, I have to satisfy myself with dreaming," she cried out, her voice reminiscent of seldom-opened doors. "If you lived as old as Bertrand Russell, you can't ever buy me a lot. The only land you can afford comes in flowerpots. What future do you have in your great university? An *emeritus* instructor, that is what you will be!"

Mr. Razon always knew when to quit. He gathered up his lecture notes, gulped down his coffee, flew out of the kitchen. Walking down the street, he began whistling snatches of melody from Beethoven's *Fifth Symphony*, somewhat recovered from his wife's outburst, indeed growing buoyant as he made his way to his lectern. There, towering above everyone else, he felt fulfilled, important, admired, appreciated, powerful, why, a virtual god on earth!

Mrs. Razon cleared up the breakfast table with cold, leashed fury. Snatching up the gold rimmed cup, her arm swung a bit wide and—thump!—she hit the percolator, and the cup's handle came off. Mr. Razon always took his coffee from that cup, yes, since they got married. She had given it to him as a wedding present. "A touch of gold for the most wonderful lips in the cosmos," her laborious inscription read. Now, looking at the handless cup, she felt terribly ashamed of her tantrum. Nevertheless, she thought, there was justification. My God, even her dreams had lost subtlety. She was sure even Sigmund Freud himself could not find any inner meaning in slabs of bacon and the lot she enclosed with violets.

Back in the old days, long before her college ring had been eroded by so much water from the kitchen faucet, she would not have dared to spit out that mouthful. To her, as with countless other students, he was a star whose light dispelled the darkness. Listening to him was an experience: the inconsequential became consequential; the unimportant, important; and the microscopic, macroscopic. She remembered as she examined the handle of the cup, which now lay on the table before her like a question mark, how her sorority sisters spun the wildest gossip to spite her for "hogging the catch of any semester."

She was sipping a Coke in the school cafeteria that day, worrying herself to pieces about the results of the prelims in logic. She could not tell an inversion from a permutation, and she thought the study of logic a plain waste of time. She was there in that university not to acquire a degree, primarily, but to save her parents from supporting a daughter for the rest of their natural lives. "Someone has got to take over," her mother said. "The richer he is, *hija*, the better for all of us."

"Why so pale and wan, my lady? Are you suffering from cosmic loneliness?" At once she knew that the voice belonged to Sir himself, the philosophy instructor. Before she could answer, she choked on her drink. Mr. Razon was himself momentarily speechless, but he sat next to her. She could feel the touch of his shirt-sleeve. To hide her shaking hands, she buried them in her voluminous skirt. "Do you know what Karl Marx would have probably said if he had seen you drinking that?" he asked, evidently not expecting an answer, for he went on quickly to other topics, one leading to another, and another. He spoke of labor—congealed capital, he said—and of the theory of surplus value, of the profit motive and the exploitative drives of men, of Adam Smith and John Locke, of laissez faire and capitalism and of imperialism and its effect on developing economies like the Philippines. "Drink then your imperialists' juice," he said at this point, raising his glass in a mock-heroic toast to her. "Let it not be said that you are ungrateful to America, the self-sacrificing champion of democracy the world over."

She got so fascinated by his dissertations, the drift of which she was not always sure she followed, that before the bell rang for the next class her hands had crawled out of their hiding places and were natural and free again.

Not long after the talk in the cafeteria, logic acquired magic and she learned enough of it to assure her of making the graduation exercises. In her black toga she looked like a widow recently bereaved. And she felt like one: Mr. Razon was nowhere to be found since the final week.

The next day while she was packing her things for the long journey home, his presence was announced by the dormitory porter. Upon hearing his name, she suddenly lifted, like a feather airborne. So light did she race down the four flights of stairs, without even panting from the exertion when she reached the parlor.

"Do you have anything important to do just now?" he said unceremoniously.

She shook her head dumbly, her happiness threatening to explode.

"Would you like to do something important?" he asked, now somewhat self-conscious, his hand rumpling his hair.

"Yes, yes, yes," she breathed.

"Well, then," Mr. Razon said as he regained command of the situation. "Change to something special and do something of importance for this cosmological ganglion before you."

Again she flew, up, up, up to her room, unaware of everything else except Mr. Razon waiting for her in the parlor. Opening her suitcase, she took out the yellow dress which was, concededly, "the killer" in her wardrobe. To make it more "deadly" she tucked in a gossamer scarf around the neckline.

The taxi stopped in front of the city hall. Mr. Razon requested her to remove her scarf from her neck and put it over her head. "You are entering hallowed ground," he explained, "where a bit of hocus-pocus will legitimize before the eyes of society what I intend to do with you."

After the civil ceremony, Mr. Razon took her to his apartment as wife. It was a small place, shrunk even more by volumes and volumes of books. When he carried her over the threshold, lecturing all the while on its significance as an act of possession, he tripped over a pile of books lying crazily on the floor. Both of them came down hard. Picking up one of the books, Mr. Razon talked to it as though it was a person. "Mad at me, Herr Schopenhauer, are you? Well, a man has to get married sometime."

Life with Mr. Razon was Graduate School in liberal education. At the breakfast table she was exposed to, then steeped in, philosophy, the humanities and the social sciences. In the beginning, she listened in wonder to him, as he expounded on various subjects. So filled with awe was she at his erudition that she could not bring herself to impinge on his intellection by bringing up such pragmatic matters as the empty rice bin a day or two before payday, and the intrusive affinal relatives who infested her domain. Besides, even if she could have mustered the courage to call his attention to these crude exigencies, she knew how he would react. The lecturer's voice would intone, "Consider the oyster, my dear. A lowly creature, isn't it? Yet, it can turn irritations into a pearl, which, as you know, is a thing of beauty. So, don't be so hasty in the consideration of irritants."

A day before their first wedding anniversary, Mr. Razon's masterpiece of a dresser set had to give way to a store-bought crib. It was with sadness that she watched it dismantled. She had grown rather fond of the apple crates with the funny mirror Mr. Razon had picked up on the sidewalks of Quiapo. "Whoever peers into this mirror shall be a creature anointed by fortune," he used to tell her as he watched her dutifully brushing her hair, steadily and with even strokes. "Not many women are afforded the splendid opportunity to visualize their portraits in the manner of a Chagall or a Modigliani. The trick in living, my dear, is to attain what the Greek stoics called 'autarky', or the development of self-sufficiency. With autarky the dark side of life can never overwhelm you."

She did not let the dark side of life overwhelm her. Not the first ten years of their life together, anyway. Transient after transient came and went. Baby after baby came and stayed. The water plant she had placed in a coffee bottle to brighten up the living room grew no more than two etiolated leaves a year. He pretended not to notice this, though. There were always the edifying talks at the breakfast table, each time sufficient unto the day. The time came, however, when backaches began to distract her, to make her listen with less than rapt attention. Then, it came down to no more than polite listening. As he analyzed the philosophy of the romantic idealists, she congratulated herself for having learned a more practical philosophy.

While Mr. Razon probed deeper and deeper into the meaning of truth, she baked and sewed for grosser profit. But the money was never enough. The children were growing. When three of them began schooling and her hands would no longer open and close freely, she could no longer ignore the etiolated plant. She now made it a point to sit and watch it, somehow taking comfort from its meagerness. Even more satisfying was her new norm of making snide remarks at the breakfast table, with malice intended, to disrupt his erudite meanderings. It was a marvel indeed to think of protein for the children when Mr. Razon was deep in metaphysical exploration.

One day Mr. Razon was discussing the problem of reality. "According to Berkeley," he began as he dropped a fried dried fish into a saucer filled with salted vinegar, "only that is real which is perceived. But perception is not limited to man. Thus, a flower in the desert is real, even if no human being is about. This is because it is perceived by God, is that not logical?"

"Sure," Mrs. Razon said, swallowing hard the bitter coffee. "I know for a fact too that our poverty may not be perceived, but it is real. No need for the Great Perceiver to make that real." With that mouthful, she strained to open her left hand, making sure that he heard the arthritic creak.

Mr. Razon was unfazed by her retort, and went on discussing Berkeley. Thoughtfully eyeing Socrates, their youngest now in kindergarten, who was busy with his bowl of gruel, he continued, "Kant did a better explanation than Berkeley. He gave the term 'phenomena' to things as they appear to the senses and the term 'noumena' to things as they are, apart from their material reality. The truly real is that which is unperceived, the *ding in sich*."

He went on and on, speaking as though to the little boy, who ignored his father's learned talk, involved as he was with the hot gruel and the pieces of dried fish floating on it like sailboats. But the boy jumped, letting go of his spoon, when mother piped up, "For God's sakes, why don't you face the phenomenon or *ding in sich*, if you wish, of our poverty?"

That night when all the children were presumed asleep, Mr. Razon asked his wife with earnest civility. "What do you want of me? I am doing the best I can. I am sorry I cannot be an Esau and exchange my birthright for a mess of pottage. Didn't you see before you married me that I am an incurable romantic? All I know is that I can only live this way."

"A life of talk? Where has it gotten you? If you are so good at it, how come you are the only one in your department untapped for a fellowship abroad? Dale Carnegie is not a profound philosopher, but I suggest you forego Nietzsche and his blond beasts and for once listen to some positive thinking."

"I don't need Dale Carnegie. You know damn well I could get a fellowship if I cared to. Woman, do you want me to believe that you, who promised to stick by me through thick and thin, would want me to commit dishonesty of the grandest proportions? While I criticize and rant against colonial miseducation, you want me to get colonial credentials and thereby participate in the perpetuation of the system?" Mr. Razon's voice must have penetrated their bedroom walls, for Immanuel started to cough persistently. He stopped short, while Mrs. Razon bustled to give the little boy comfort.

In December of the year she began talking back at breakfast, Immanuel died. After he was buried in a coffin provided by friends, the breakfast table became quiet. Mr. Razon ate his breakfast without a word while Mrs. Razon went over the classified ads page, where she now reposed her hopes for better times. There was hardly any job she could fit into. The business world apparently had no need for a woman rushing headlong into her climacteric. As soon as she realized this awful truth, she began reading the page for amusement. She would examine all the advertisements on real estate. In no time at all she was a walking quote board of real estate prices.

One afternoon while all the children were in school, Mrs. Razon was as usual engaged in her favorite pastime. In her mind, she was building a new house. Should she use granulithic flooring, or would it be terrazo tiles? She was considering the advantage of terrazo tiles against the advice of her architect when she was rudely interrupted by Mr. Razon, announcing, "I have quit the university."

"Say that again slowly," she said, calmly, still unbelieving.

"I have quit the university," Mr. Razon said in tones befitting the Hegelian opening, "History is becoming."

Mr. Razon took fat pay envelopes from his new job. In no time at all, Mrs. Razon was able to pay the down payment on a lot in a first-class subdivision where mercury lights turned night into day. Month by month as she amortized the lot, changes took shape in the rented apartment. The breakfast table had ceased to be a lectern for edifying and uplifting talk. What passed for conversation, most often, contributed greatly to indigestion. Mrs. Razon usually started the ball rolling with little reminders on the need to save and scrimp so that the Torrens title of the lot would soon be in her hands. The children, whose interest in food had been diverted to more urgent commodities, became savages. They turned mealtimes into gripe sessions. "Why am I not getting this?" "Why am I not getting that?"

On the rare occasions that Mr. Razon managed to eat with his family, he would softly speak of commitment to self. "Man has only one life to live. It is imperative for him to live it well. He must never betray himself by being untrue to himself." Whenever he spoke thus, his eyes would wander far, far away, and he did not hide his hands clenching into tight fists which shook as though from intense pain.

While Mr. Razon racked his brain in search of the elusive, if not delusive, words to sell a product, Mrs. Razon rocked herself to dreamland in her rocking chair. As she swayed to and fro, details would fall into place to form the dream-house she would have on her partially owned lot. The longer Mr. Razon stayed up in his office, the more intricate and particular the details became. She chose with care and capriciousness. She was never satisfied. Her house and garden suffered from frequent alterations. Tall trees with shade enough to cool a whole house gave way to ornamental bushes, all in a moment's flight of fancy. The escritoire where Mr. Razon was to write his *magnum opus* someday, when the toil for money would come to an end, journeyed from place to place in the house, in search of privacy and proper lighting. The antique collection, which she had purchased in past daydreams became highly mobile, so mobile, in fact, sometimes, that the constant movement hypnotized her, sending her dozing in her chair.

One day in June while she was thus preoccupied, Mr. Carlos materialized in front of her rocking chair. From the very way he stood awkwardly before her, she could tell that he had come on an errand that had something to do with Mr. Razon. "Did he quit his job?" she asked, panic starting to tint her voice. Mr. Carlos did not answer. With unsteady hands he touched her shoulders, as though to bid her to stand, and when she did, he led her to the company car which was waiting outside her door. ✿

Grief

Caroline S. Hau

MRS. JIA had seen her husband operate the grinder many times. She knew what had to be done.

Pouring the steaming beans into the receptacle, she carefully adjusted the axis of the two table-sized grindstones that were stacked together on a slab—monstrous stones that crushed and ground and yet seemed imperturbably immobile. Taking firm hold of the enormous wooden pole that projected from one of the stones, Mrs. Jia began to push. Rotating the grindstones had not seemed so difficult at first. But the night was oppressively warm, humid, and as the moonrays pierced through the indigo clouds heavy with rain, Mrs. Jia began to feel that the wooden pole was getting harder and harder to push after each turn. Her heavy breathing turned into muted pants. Dark patches appeared and spread under the armpits and on the upper front and back of her old shirt. Mrs. Jia's arm muscles tightened considerably, and she felt a slight strain on her back. But she continued to work, pausing only to wipe the sweat from her eyes.

When she saw that the beans were ground enough, she collected the remaining bean dregs into large flour bags, and squeezed and pounded them to extract the fluid. The sight of the milky white soya juice flowing out of the grinder, trickling from the bags, gave her some satisfaction. Mrs. Jia's arms throbbed with each pounding. After a while, the rhythm of her hands began to echo in her mind like some tribal drum, relentless, emptying the brain of all thoughts and sensations except the pounding of the bags. Though her body trembled from sheer strain, the pain meant nothing to her.

Mrs. Jia finished grinding the day's quota of yellow beans earlier than she anticipated. The little ones were not asleep yet. She sat down and shared her supper with them. She ate quickly, sparingly. She had had to ration the food for each meal. The children always seemed to be hungry, even though they had eaten their supper. Mrs. Jia did not mind that she could only eat twice a day, once in early morning, once at night. She was not going to starve, and she would do anything for the little ones. She still had so many things to do this evening, and work invariably took her mind off hunger. But her appetite had not been good anyway.

When the eldest asked her about Father, Mrs. Jia carefully put down the pitcher of water and told him that his Papa had some important business to take care of so he could not come home today. No, she did not know when he would finish his work, but she was sure that he would come home right away after he had taken care of things.

He said not to worry, Mrs. Jia said.

There was still time to scrub the floor and wash some of the dirty laundry after Mrs. Jia had washed the plates and set away a plate of choice viands for the little ones' Papa, in case he came home. Afterwards, she tucked the little ones to bed and went to the kitchen.

Mrs. Jia cooked the soya amid the whistling steam of kettles and cauldrons. She made soya milk, *tao-hue*, and dried bean curd. While the *tao-hue* curdled on the pan and the bean curd nestled beneath a huge heavy rock, Mrs. Jia poured soya milk into clean whiskey bottles. There was plenty to sell in the morning.

Everything was now wrapped and packed in the baskets.

Mrs. Jia scrubbed the dirt and sweat of a night's work from her hair and body. It felt so good to settle down on the rocking chair in the living room. The stillness of the night wrapped itself like a blanket about her. She saw today's newspaper on the little table in front of her rocking chair, loudly proclaiming another Japanese victory. The lulling motion of the chair gave her a sense of ease so that even the headline meant nothing to her.

Beside the newspaper was her husband's pipe. Mrs. Jia looked at it for a long time. She saw smoke curling from the receptacle. She saw her husband's calloused hands absently rubbing the mahogany. She smelled burnt tobacco. She heard smacking lips and fingernails tapping against the bdy of the pipe in unconscious rhythm.

Mrs. Jia smiled, then suddenly leant over and picked up the pipe. It smelled very faintly of burnt tobacco. She touched the smooth mahogany length of it, then rubbed her fingerprints from the receptacle with her shirt.

Where was he now?

The rocking motion quickened. Mrs. Jia found herself still staring at the pipe.

Everything had happened so suddenly. One moment, out of the corner of her eye, Mrs. Jia saw the bare back of her husband in the courtyard, glistening in the moonlight with sweat, and she heard the harsh friction of the grindstones like crunching gravel at each rotating motion. Mrs. Jia was waiting for the beans to boil, and steam had already clouded the kitchen when, all in a moment's time, her husband was there beside her. hair plastered to his skull leathery in the lamplight, small black eyes dripping sweat and lips pressed thin and white.

I must go, he said to her. They need men to dig some more ditches.

Mrs. Jia had to run to look out the kitchen door to the courtyard. She saw them, smoking cigarettes, braying hoarsely at something which one of them was saying, a jabber of vowels that meant nothing to her. Beside them the grinder stood silent, immobile, and half of the day's quota of soya juice darkened the reddish earth. And above, the long slivers of their bayonets glinted in the evening light.

Do not worry, she heard her husband say, his slight form blocking them from view. Take care of things while I am gone.

Mrs. Jia had stood by the kitchen door until they had all gone, until her husband's sweat-stained red shirt was seen no more. Then she stepped into the courtyard, picked up the overturned pail, scraped the crushed beans out of the grind stones and into the pail.

She started all over again.

For Mrs. Jia, it had suddenly seemed important to move around, to work. The rhythmic monotony and the dull pain of her muscles produced nothingness. And every night, Mrs. Jia would wait for the intoxicating numbness to soothe her pulsating temples and hot dry eyes. In her mind, she often saw the monolithic grey stones of the grinder oozing milk-white juice from their dark crevice.

Mrs. Jia ceased rocking. With infinite care, she replaced the pipe in its position, got up and, feeling the weight of her limbs, walked to the bedroom.

"Tao-hue, tao-kua, tao-hu!"

"Tao-hue, tao-kua, tao-hu!"

The baskets of bean curd bouncing at the end of the bamboo pole slung on the shoulder and a hand grasping the cauldron of *tao-hue*. Mrs. Jia walked towards the row of houses which stood facing the plaza.

She felt light-hearted for once. The weight of her merchandise had lessened considerably. In a way, she had them to thank for the brisk business. Ever since they came, there had been a shortage of grain. Prices were shooting sky-high, and no one was eating rice anymore.

Of course her husband had his regular clients, but Mrs. Jia felt sure that another round would fetch new buyers. With luck, she could sell everything by noon. Mrs. Jia was already thinking about what she was going to buy at the market later. Maybe fruit for the little ones (especially the youngest, who was sickly), a few yards of cloth... and, yes, tobacco for her husband.

Half-way to the plaza, Mrs. Jia seemed to stumble. She saw one of them standing near the entrance, bayonet glinting icily in the morning light. It was too late to turn back. Mrs. Jia could not see what he looked like (nor had she any desire to find out), but she saw him stiffen at her approach, just a slight tensing of the back that almost immediately unwound. Nobody roamed the streets this early, and Mrs. Jia was alone.

She was glad that she looked inconspicuous in a straw hat, loose blue shirt and nondescript skirt which revealed a pair of her husband's oldest trousers at the calves. Yet when she came to stand some distance from him, she was unable to swallow.

She bowed before him, seeing shiny black boots, ironed khaki trousers and the point of the bayonet.

The harsh sounds he uttered she could not understand. For one hideous moment, she thought he wanted her to come closer, or that he wanted her bean curd. Her hand clenched around the bamboo pole.

It was a sign of dismissal, after all. A brusque wave of the hand, and she crept away to the nearest house.

She found that she had to sit down for a while. She was breathing hard. There was no relief. A knot had formed within her when she made her obeisance. She saw the red shirt of her husband's, dark in those areas where moisture had stained them, then her mind went blank. Her eyes burned. She wanted to hurt and claw, do something violent to ease the pain of her hot dry eyes and the knot of sudden despair that was choking her. The smell of the bean curd nauseated her. Soon she was retching near the gutter, but nothing came out. Her stomach was empty.

It was almost noon when Mrs. Jia, wan and weary, stopped by her neighbor's. It was oppressively hot. Things swam before Mrs. Jia's eyes, and everywhere she went, she heard people say they wished that rain would finally fall, for rain had not fallen for a long time.

Mrs. Ong promised to buy the last batch of bean curd from Mrs. Jia. Upon the woman's insistence, Mrs. Jia reluctantly accepted a cup of substitute coffee in the kitchen. Mrs. Ong, fat and talkative, chattered away about the humid weather. But there was a hurried, whispered exchange between the two women that had something to do with the latest rumor of a surprise attack on the part of the Resistance. Mrs. Ong seemed to know everything that was happening here. Where she got her information Mrs. Jia had no idea.

From her, Mrs. Jia learned that another neighbor, Mrs. Li's husband, had just been taken away for questioning.

They think he is passing information. Mrs. Ong whispered into Mrs. Jia's ear.

Where is Anna right now? asked Mrs. Jia. She is with me, upstairs. She is beside herself with worry. She refuses to eat.

Does she cry all the time? Mrs. Jia asked. Yes, of course. Who wouldn't? After all, if you ask me, I do not think it is a mild affair, do you? He might not come home again.

Mrs. Jia felt herself tremble. And her little ones? They're safe with the grandmother, said Mrs. Ong. Anna is inconsolable, simply inconsolable. And, by the way, do you know that Ah-Lo's bakery has been shut down? They say...

Mrs. Ong stopped. Mrs. Jia looked up and saw a woman whose hair hung in untidy strands about her face, contorted like some tribal dance mask. Her eyes were streaming.

Mrs. Jia backed away and allowed Mrs. Ong to take charge. The woman's sobs were like dry rasping coughs. Mrs. Ong was crooning as to a child. Mrs. Jia could not understand what she was saying.

It occurred to Mrs. Jia that the woman was Mrs. Li. But this woman who was weeping with abandon could not have been Mrs. Li, whom Mrs. Jia always saw as a dry middle-aged woman who would have remained untouched by any calamity.

In truth, seeing the crying woman frightened Mrs. Jia. She did not know what to do. It had only tightened the knot within her, the knot she sought to loosen through nothingness. Hers was a different kind of pain. It scalded her bowels and burned her eyes, but it could not come out. Mrs. Jia found herself unable to console.

She had never brought herself to examine the pain within. She had never been one to lose hope, and she was not going to lose it now. She had to be strong. But it was not enough to merely set away some food each night, only to let the little ones eat it in the morning. Even the nothingness could not stem the growing weariness, the heaviness planted by her husband's absence.

Mrs. Jia was tired of it all—the constant waiting, the empty space in the bed, her lies fed to the little ones.

She stumbled out of Mrs. Ong's house and like a blind woman sought her courtyard. The sight of the grinder standing immovable awoke in her vision of its dark crevice bleeding milk-white soya. She wanted to see the juice flow, as she had seen many times.

She held the pole with shaking hands and pushed. The grating sound was there. But the crevice was dry. There were no steaming beans to crush and grind. Belatedly, Mrs. Jia realized her foolishness. She let go of the pole and sank to the reddish earth, leaning against the grinder until her cheek touched its grey hard roughness. It was hot. But Mrs. Jia felt no pain. She was waiting for the other pain of her hot dry eyes to subside.✿

Old Day Today

Edith L. Tiempo

> *It has become now*
> *A thing like the stars,*
> *Neither yours nor mine,*
> *Glittering, quivering in the wind.*
>
> > —From Chung Han-mo,
> > as translated by Ko Won

> ...dusty gardener,
> are you
>
> alive yet,
> do I live on yet, in your gray
>
> considering eye
>
> > —"A Figure of Time," Denise Levertov

IN THE twilight Mr. Patron walked through the grilled iron gate and up the path lined on both sides with flowers blooming profusely in huge clay pots; a shock of purple bougainvillae and yellow and white chrysanthemums and gold and red roses alternated with the maculate red-and-green mayanas and the yellow and maroon crotons with their random speckles blurred together in the daylight already turned to grey. Celina, the maid, was busy with the sprinkler. Mr. Patron opened the front door of his home and stepped inside, standing quietly for a short moment under the high ceiling of the living room as he fitted his eyes to the dusk. The lights had not yet been turned on. Chirping sounds, high and rusty, and infinitely sleepy, streamed into the house from outside the glass louvers. The cicadas had started their evening rounds in the tall avocado and mango trees around the house.

In the far room his daughter Lis was talking to her baby girl and he was momentarily amused hearing the light bright voice and her careful slowed-down way of speaking. Lis reserved the voice and the manner for the baby and the five blonde dolls that seemed always to be surrounding the child whenever she played.

Mr. Patron turned on the ceiling lights in the living room and the dining room.

"I don't see your mother," he called. "Is she home?"

"Dad? You're late today." Lis had switched to her somewhat husky lower-register. "No, Mom isn't home yet. She's at the old house."

From the open door of the room he saw Lis on the floor and his granddaughter in the playpen, holding on to a toy. The way with all infants, he thought, their fat little hands gripped things with authority. In the child's clutch was Curious George the toy monkey. It was clearly a more interesting personality than any in the circle of yellow-headed lassies, contemplating her with their identical pretty stares. Come to think of it, Mr. Patron mused, no wonder the child preferred Curious George. He stood at the door and made small absent noises at his granddaughter by way of greeting, and the child responded, chortling and lifting the monkey's face at him, inviting him to share whatever mysterious comfort she found in the unlikely toy.

To Lis he said mildly, "You should have asked Celina to go with your mother. She shouldn't be there by herself at this hour." He muttered, "The wharf area is a rough place at any time."

"I know, Dad. Not the slum people, it's the bums and the thieves. All kinds of tough characters roaming around there." She said, looking at him, "I wish there was a storehouse on the wharf to rent. Too bad we have to use the first floor of the old house for a granary."

Mr. Patron looked resigned; the idea had, of course, occurred to the family before. He turned away and a small gusty sigh escaped him before he could suppress it. In the privacy of the living room he gave way to his irritation and allowed his face to show exactly what he felt, a husband's extreme annoyance and frustration, with a wife he had spent the last ten of their thirty-five years learning not to incite to argument. Could any man reason with a wife who refused to argue? He wished Jenny would leave the corn shipment to their son—and Pete himself had often told her, "It's no place for a woman, Mom!" Pete had urged her,

"Let's pay a *bantay*, maybe one of the tenants, and he can stay at night on the upper floor. Just so somebody would be there."

Mr. Patron remembered how Jenny fell silent and had set her preoccupied look on them, a familiar phenomenon which their son hastened to meet with his own argument, "What's the extra expense, hey, Mom? It's only after the corn is milled and bagged; anyway until the bags are brought from the storehouse to the ship."

But it was a foregone conclusion. Jenny had left the room and Terio told his son, "You've got to take it philosophically. Especially when it's women you deal with."

"Good thing you taught philosophy, too, Dad. Gives you a certain attitude."

Pete was flippantly referring to the two weeks when his father had taken over a philosophy class at the divinity school. The regular professor went on sick leave and because no one else was available, Mr. Patron had allowed himself to be talked into taking over. It was now a family joke—he had made no secret of the disconcerting experience. A lawyer's philosophy was mostly home-grown and not much equipment for a theology class.

Anyway, Jenny had pretended inattention to their son's idea, as he knew she would. She'd be losing an excuse to go up to the old house, and he knew that as much as the corn it was also that she had to see the place every so often. It had belonged to her parents, dead many years ago, even before Lis and Pete were born. Jenny's mother had inherited it from her own father, Lolo Matias, Jenny's grandfather. It meant something, Jenny's attachment, perhaps to a childhood she had lost not really to the passage of time, which was acceptable, but more because of its peculiar ravages upon the neighborhood where she grew up. For the old place had been a part of a once-exclusive area fronting the sea, until the wharf encroached upon the affluent houses and displaced one after another of the group of small but almost regal structures, some of wood and cement, but most of them brick and stone. And the square sheds and grey storehouses gradually dislodged courtyard, hall, azotea, pavilion, atrium, the vine-covered balustraded balconies, the colonnaded entrances and arcades over passageways, the arabesqued walls and cornices, until the growing waterfront slum neighborhood looked as though it had always been there. Of course it was Time, but it was more the salt in the sea winds dampening and corroding with rust, first, the costly furnishing, and then the elegant nineteenth-century houses, until the owners' descendants gave up the fight and the wrecking crews came in and whatever could be saved was trundled away. A few years ago Jenny had the wall built around the house and lot, and beside the iron gate she had a painted sign set up: GENOVEVA ARGUELLES PATRON. NO TRESPASSING.

He was deciding to go after her when they heard Herman's motorbike outside and his son-in-law came in, bringing with him the windblown impression of a fast and dusty ride.

Herman always came trailing a strong evocation of sustained and healthy activity out in the open, although recently his new duties at the radio station kept him mainly indoors, he was programming a new series of vernacular plays. He doffed his helmet and laid it in its usual place on the shelf by the door. For a tall and brawny fellow he moved his body—his head, arms and torso—in a quick and precise way, like a sprinter slowing down.

"I brought Mom home, Dad." He sounded brisk too, and unwearied, where one expected some show of tiredness. The radio station was after all set up at the transmitter site two towns away, and Herman did spend part of his regular schedule motorbiking around the countryside getting on-the-spot interviews with the farmers, the barrio teachers and barangay officers. "She's still outside instructing Celina. About the Shastas, I think she said."

The house was taking on the coziness that came at evening with the return of everyone. The voices no longer sounded fragile and solitary but rose, murmurous inside the room, or overlapped and blended together; the odors of cooking meat stew and steaming rice warmed the air.

Soon after, Jenny Patron came in, a slightly built woman in her late fifties or early sixties, looking just now a little tired. The dark eyes were deeply set and brooding under the neat arched brows, and the curved lashes still edged her eyes in a thick fringe. She looked fastidious and withdrawn, until one noticed the strong jaws and her thin mouth, the pink elongated lips that were habitually pressed tightly together.

"I'm sorry, Terio, I didn't think it was late, it got dark so fast." She explained, "I was looking around. I think the old house needs some repairs." She gave her husband a quick peck on the cheek and glanced through the closed screen door of the kitchen, where the other maid was winding up the last bits for supper, some sliced raw vegetables on a tray, carrots, cucumbers, a sweet turnip. The good smell of the stewed meat whiffed out of the kitchen as the pan was uncovered and the stew poured into a bowl. Jenny looked at her husband, her palm on the screen door as though she had forgotten to open it. "Leaks in the roof, Terio, the ceiling has started to bulge in two places." She dropped her hand from the screen and mimed with her two hands to show the size of the bulging spots. She shook her head. "And two other places, some bad warps on a wall panel in the sala."

Her husband was shaking his head vigorously, clearly signalling his displeasure. "I think you should leave that to us. Always more and more repairs, the way with these old houses." He said, summoning patience, "Jenny, look, there are three men in this house, after all."

Some of the tiredness had left her. Whenever she sensed an argument her face took on a familiar distracted expression, that kind of look that was abruptly effective, like a harsh protest or a screech. Without another word she pushed through the door and quickly escaped into the kitchen.

Pete was the last to come home. He came in the car, which his father hardly ever used. Pete needed the car; the college where he had just started teaching was on the far end of town and one had to cross the bridge over the Ipon River to get there. His father took the bicycle or chose to walk home, as he did that afternoon, the law office was just five blocks away. Pete was long-boned like his father, and they both stood tall, with good shoulders and narrow sturdy trunks. He got his heavy-lashed eyes from his mother, but the sudden smile, and his ready laugh and robust good nature were entirely his own. Seven years younger than his sister, he made Lis seem tiny when she happened to be standing beside him.

"Evening, everybody," he said, setting his books on the nearest shelf, and almost in the same breath, "Hey, that smells good, what's for supper?"

In the clear morning sunshine Jenny stood on the path to the gate and watched the retreating figure of Terio wheeling away down the street on his bicycle. She thought with pride, no one would know he was just two years short of seventy. He had promised often and loudly and emphatically to quit, but only when he could retire into another job, different, but work he liked. "Something for the hands— yeoman's work, Jenny," she recalled his boisterous promise whenever the subject came up. Except, Jenny thought regretfully, except that Terio was just not a farmer. She admitted to herself that, of the two of them, she had often had to control the more restless, perhaps the more reckless tendencies. The family insisted she level off her activities, but no one was surprised, nor happy, when she decided to continue looking after the thirty-five hectares of flat land in Libgos, twelve kilometers away—and she had not even told anyone yet of the projected piggery, that was how she planned to make use of the low shelf of land that was lying idle. She anticipated a clamor about the piggery—get the tenants to do it, they'd insist and evoke again the incident of two years ago which had turned out to be harmless heart murmurs.

She turned aside into the garden. It was cool and still under the sparse foliage of the frangipani and champaka. The air felt thin this morning and the sky was cloudless, a pale aqua streaked with grey stains like fine dust settling down. Hardly any wind, just a half-hearted breeze jogging the tops of the taller fern trees into the barest of nodding movements. More and more these days she liked to stop in the garden before getting on to the bills and receipts, and phoning in the little orders for the farm—a sack of feed, a can of paint, a new hurricane lamp for the hen house. It was as though she needed the long minute in the garden to prepare for a pell-mell run. She stood momentarily still and closed her eyes, thinking of the small stirrings in the soil under her feet, the business of creating life and nourishing it in a constant quiet fever deep underground, heat and coolness fanning furiously through the pockets of air among the roots, the sap rising through the veins of the tree trunks and stems and into the leaves. It all seemed so uncontrived but, of course, there was a fearfully strict rhythm to these processes. Through her closed lids the sun filtered and on her feet it shifted and spun and she felt penetrated like a plant by the light and the air, felt the plant sap rising from the earth and up her legs and coursing through her body's tissues in cold waves; her feet were rooted fast, her mind frozen in the long minute shared with the green growing vegetation in all the gardens everywhere. Then the coldness converged on her, and between the quiet air and the fever underground was no longer any barrier of earth, and the coolness was turning the upper world into stream-water, cutting cold swaths of oblivion around her and through her. She half-dreamed and half-dreaded drowning in the rising flood. Shivering she moved to shake off the clinging filaments of cold air and water and light.

She moved automatically and her steps led her forward, as they almost always did, to the long rows of shelves crowded with the pots of African violets. Dozens of them blossomed in small pots and there were more of them in bigger clay ewers and small wide-mouthed plastic basins, to allow for leafier spread. She wondered again at the way the diminutive flower heads were clustered in the center of each pot. They were like exotic cauliflowers mutated by some quirk of nature, by a strange conjunction of light and temperature, and air and water and the densities of darkness under the soil. They sat in their pots, the flower coronets, glowing with excessive colors against the green furry leaves. When the familiar lurch in her chest came it didn't come as an abrupt jerk to call her attention, but rather like a breath moving gently, snagged in her ribs, prowling there like a live thing, a breath pulling, pulling free, and suddenly exploding there, splitting her open. In that instant she longed for the cold trancelike dream that had swamped her a few minutes before, and her hand reached out blindly, the palm drifting down like a feather or an antenna on the nearest pot of violets. A mindless act, but it checked her agitation, as if the vivid colors had the power to flow into her hand like some steadying drug, and into her sinews, up into her head... What gruesome osmosis was this that sucked in colors, too? And what of these fantasies coming each time as a shaking force and quickly gone? She had been having the curious moments of daydreaming for some time, when she had been by herself in the farm, or in the old house, and right there in the garden. She had told no one, not even Lis, about the strange long minute coming one after another, for she knew that the summons came partly from her own self, and that each time, she had invited a challenge from the forces that could be both malevolent and good.

From the neighbor's yard across the street came the sounds of garden scissors clipping away. *Click...Click-*

Click...Click. That was Fidel. The Figueroas' occasional gardener was trimming the ivy hedge fronting the street. Through the loop designs of her own garden wall she could see Fidel standing on the far edge of the lane, flourishing the scissors. He had his back to her and was almost on tiptoe reaching up to snip the vines on the upper part of the fence. Careful and systematic, he had worked the scissors in a progressive horizontal line from the middle part of the wall, going up; then later, going down, she supposed.

Jenny Patron stared. Looking at Fidel she could be looking at the old gardener in her parents' home clipping away at the shrubbery. Asiong, that gardener, was Fidel's father, Fidel was his son; Fidel was also a gardener and himself a father to three grown sons. Once upon a time... once upon a short time ago the boy Fidel with the round black eyes and spindly legs chased after dragonflies in the sunshine, across the yard of the old house—impossible that he could be the middle-aged man across the lane. Black button eyes, sticks for legs, a high screech, streaky fingers closed about a stone or a half-eaten fruit... Somehow she was glad it was only his straight hard back she saw. Somehow she was fiercely glad she wasn't looking at his face.

"Mom?" Lis broke into her silence and Jenny turned around. Little Peb, a toddler for a couple of months now, was breaking free of her mother's hand. The child's look darted away to a large clump of bachelor's buttons, where once or twice before, Lis had taken her away from her aggressive exploration of the interesting mound of lavender and green: *What could it be, a giant Humpty-Dumpty in a flower suit?*

"Could you keep her with you for just a short time, Mom? I'm going to the Bookdale for a couple of books." She added contritely, "Did I interrupt something?"

"No, nothing, really." Jenny thought, and it's the truth, too, because it even seemed that Lis and the little girl were brought there as almost a logical consequence, drawn by her mind's freakish bending with the pull and thrust of time that was fluid and erratic, and the rather improvident turn of her memories.

"Come, Pebbles," Jenny took the child's hand. "I think we see eye to eye about those bachelor's buttons."

Lis watched them, the grandma getting the child to pluck a cautious handful, taking their time about it, picking each purple button with judicious care.

"Wait," Lis said. She left quickly and returned with a folded mat. Slipping the sling bag off her shoulder she held the mat by the edge and lifted wide her arms, shaking the mat open and looking flushed with the little exertion. She found a good place and spread it on the corner where the grass was thick and deep. "You can both sit there when *Lola* and you get tired picking flowers," she told the unlistening Pebbles. "Time for your snap soon, too."

"Hurry back," Jenny said, noting with approval her daughter's still youthful figure, the long legs and swift springy steps, high heels clicking on the flagstoned path to the gate. Her storybook daughter, she thought, and the metaphor seemed justified, seeing what a near thing it had been, having Lis at thirty-two and Pete at thirty-nine.

To what did a person commit himself when he multiplied his life by becoming a parent? For herself she learned early how the children could be like the things of the world, they could be too dear and too close, comfortable perhaps for her and Terio, but for her children, what?—an extended playpen? a benign yoke? And so she had taken pride in giving them freedom and more freedom even when they were children, caring that the guiding halter would not chafe; and it had always been instinctive self-protection, too, how she looked at them as her extensions but also as absolutely separate people who could cut loose at any time. For all that, they were very much her children. Strange how the legal term was the most physically and emotionally accurate. Not just *children* or *offspring*, but *issues*. From her insides. See how Pete's features borrowed from her and Terio, and yet his temperament was something else. Both children, in fact. Set deeply in their brisk and hardy good nature was a capricious fusion, fey and almost willful, a heedless tendency to dream fused with a trigger-temper. It was a combination mostly unsuspected even by them. How did they get their buried traits, not from their parents, but from a grandfather they hadn't even seen? Potenciano Arguelles; there lurked a bit of him in her children and no one else could do anything about it. Besides, latent traits were too much like sleeping dogs to be lightly provoked.

Pebbles was getting restless. She had dropped her bunch of flowers.

"Time-out, okey?" Jenny led the child to the wide mat on the grass, calling out to Celina to bring Pebbles' little bottle of calamansi juice.

At the supper table Herman was holding forth on a new concern: artistic responsibility. Herman was a quiet man. But he got seized by fits of indignation about people who were born with all their mental equipment intact (as he put it), but who acted mulish and stupid. His personal ire often shaded off into a more abstract interest but usually he was censuring the unreliability of artists as people; the unreliability of his artist-cousin Caloy, in particular. Herman thought it a kind of betrayal that the artists' steadiness as workmen should be a precarious matter whenever their work happened to be intended as "utilitarian" items: paintings, sculpture, figurines for office rooms, foyers, convention halls and such. Artists were not exempted from pure toil, they were expected to hack away at a mundane job as everybody else did—although the artists tended to think otherwise.

"Of course," Herman said, "Caloy would rather paint an abstract; or a portrait, maybe. Every artist itches to do that, he'd rip his guts for a chance to do that. But the bank's been waiting for his piece of garden scenery—it's really a mural for that wide panel back of the tellers—and Caloy has been balking."

It seemed the bank manager had privately transmitted his grievance to Herman, knowing Caloy was his cousin.

"What does Caloy have against the mural?" Pete wanted to know.

Lis asked curiously, "How do students get contrary? I mean apart from the usual laziness."

Peter affected a disenchanted snicker. "What do you call it when a student says a trope 'could be some kind of circus equipment'? Probably he means a kind of cross between a rope and a trampoline. *Ergo*, trope."

Here Terio came into the conversation and he was very much the ex-magistrate, pontificating crisply, "That's how it goes. Not surprising. Man will be man."

Lis the curious one said, "And that means what, Dad?"

"Just that man has been at it for thousands of years. Naturally outrageous and contrary, and trying for perfection, but it's slow going. Or simply no go at all, maybe; could be a hopeless job. We've been at it long enough."

"You mean, Dad," said Herman, "perhaps like one of my nice resolutions—something like, I cut cigarettes one month and then sneak up on it, and back to full puffing in another month."

"Or my secret tippling, Dad, although it's just one beer at the corner store," said Pete.

"I'm not the one to complain about human orneriness," Terio told them. "I still earn my livelihood on people's contrary nature. But we are all more durable than we think. Perhaps because everyone knows he has to live, no matter what." He was enjoying himself, sounding off, sagacious, mock-ominous, "And he has to live with his inability to cope with the final obstacle, his flesh, infernal thing. It dies."

Jenny looked at them. "It's built into things," she said vaguely, and made another isolated remark. "This morning I saw Fidel, the Figueroas' gardener. Or rather, I saw his back."

They looked at her questioningly. "I didn't see his face," she explained. "It's all wrinkled up, of course, at his age."

Lis couldn't say exactly why but she thought her mother had made a relevant statement, somehow.

The cargo boat for Cebu was expected from Mindanao in two days, but no matter, the last of the corn crop had come in from the mill and had been brought to the storehouse by the wharf. Since it was Saturday afternoon and Pete was free he drove his mother to the old house, promising to come back for her later, in about an hour. She had brought a basket with her, the oranges from the tree in the yard were ready to pick. The tree was a species called Jerusalem orange—said to be native to the hills of Judea and was the kind that didn't grow tall. She intended to pick the oranges herself.

Jenny closed the rusty gate behind her but did not padlock it, although she hesitated because of the group of noisy young fellows playing some kind of catchball at the side of the house. They were playing just outside the wall. She usually gave them wide berth, these nervy excitable children quickly up in arms at a slight or fancied offense. So prickly, she thought, was that sort of dignity they had to keep intact. She left the gate unlocked—anyway, it was three o'clock; it wasn't as if it was already dark, when she would have to look out for prowlers.

She made a cursory inspection around the granary, checking briefly on the sacks of milled corn piled halfway up to the ceiling. Satisfied that mice had not invaded the place she locked the door and climbed the stairs. On the upper floor the air was dry and smelled of desiccated mushrooms, the smell of a really old house that had been left empty for a long time. The air, the dust was close and stale. She stopped in the living room and slid open a tall window panel to the side. From the opening a wide band of sunlight pushed into the room, so that she stood in its glaring brightness.

From the partially opened window she had almost a whole view of the waterfront. Outside the fence the group of boys had become noisier and their screaming momentarily unnerved her; it seemed too much of a reminder that the neighborhood she had walled out was pressing its way in. The putrid little huts that were the boys' homes stood on stagnant water; the scum thickened around the low posts; a whole squalid block of them before they gave way to the looming grey buildings of the pier. The many children who had spilled out of the huts like frenzied mice kept running out into the street, not minding the crammed lorries and cargo trucks speeding down to the end of the wharf. Three greasy interisland freighters heaved beside the piles and two foreign liners were moored a little farther out at sea. As she leaned on the sill she felt the quick throb inside her chest, something she knew did not have much to do with the functioning of her heart or her other vital organs, but with what she was thinking about or felt, the emotion intensifying in a kind of abstract takeover, a willful tendency of her system which over the years she had lost the ability to isolate or control. It happened when people were becoming one with the elements, she thought, for she herself had grown incapable of restraining, or warding off involvements with matters uncertain or unpredictable, and could not try consistently enough to blunt her sensibilities when they encroached in the form of people and what happened to them. It used to be easy, a reflex, the valve that shut off whatever one would not endure. But people lost the instinct and soon could not judge when even trivial and innocent contacts could betray.

Outside, the boys abruptly stopped their play and their concerted shrieks tore into the air; the ball had vanished over the wall and landed in the weeds and the tall grass in her yard. Weren't they a little old to be playing catchball? She observed that they ranged in age from about twelve to—eighteen? The two big boys were at least that age. One of them was a square-faced strapping fellow, who rushed into the yard after pushing open the gate panels without ceremony, and plunged into the tall grass, where he rooted around in the weeds.

"Not with your hands, you fool! There may be snakes. Get a stick." Jenny's shout of warning jerked him upright and she saw at once she had frightened him. Not about the snakes but because he had obviously not seen her at the window when he came barging into the yard. His startled face was lifted at her and she saw his outrage and humiliation at being frightened off his guard. He gave her a horrible grin and raised his fists.

"Old witch!" he bellowed. "It's *our* ball, so what? Old witch! old witch!" The others outside took it up, mostly to dissipate their own fright. "Old witch, old witch!"—howling and prancing like savages working up to a kill.

Jenny slammed the panel closed and leaned against it. She was shaking and angry with herself for feeling unstrung. What was there so repulsive about this kind of cruel play? Sickening, the kind of fear thrown at her by these boys. How did it get distorted and mindless? She cowered against the window, fighting down her feelings of repugnance and distress. The voices outside had toned down. They had found the ball.

In the dimness of the sala she became aware of a shape coming out of one of the far rooms, a small shape, and it moved so quietly she had no chance to be alarmed. A little boy. She thought, about five or six. When her eyes got used to the dusk beyond the living room she saw he was older, ten or eleven. He came nearer and was now in the middle of the room and just a few steps away from her.

"I heard them," he said in a voice incongruously low and full. She had expected a thin and reedy treble. "I thought they would come up here and harm you."

"How did you get here?"

"They sent me. When you were down in the granary. I am told to watch you when they'll be throwing the big sticks at the star apple tree outside the window, to drop the ripe ones."

"They should have asked me."

"It's outside your wall. And you don't care for the fruit, anyway. The ripe ones just fall and rot."

He scratched idly at his arm, dislodging the strap of his dirty outsized sandow, so that it dangled from one shoulder.

"You are not a witch, are you?"

"What makes you think I am?"

"We were talking about that. Some of them said you must be a witch because you are old but not wrinkled or toothless."

She came forward slowly. He did not move or turn away. She stopped and they faced each other. He stared at her and explained, "They said a young-looking old woman was sure to be a witch."

"But you're not afraid of me?"

"No." He opened his hand. On the palm was a little round pebble. "It protects me. From ghosts and witches."

She found nothing to say to this and he went on, "Also you have to threaten the witch first, before she could try anything."

Jenny laughed then, and was surprised at how easily she had become relaxed. She noticed that the boys outside were quiet for the moment.

"You have a name, of course. What is it?"

Fear leaped into the grimy face. "Why do you want to know?"

"I have a name, it's on the sign beside the gate. What's yours?"

But she never heard it. A heavy piece of wood crashed against the wall outside. The boy gave a loud cry as another length of wood intended for the star apple tree was hurled against the side of the house. The stick tore through the moldered wooden wall, hit her on the side of the head, and she fell to her knees, feeling the room sway and spin. From far away she thought she heard the boy screaming, and then the thud of many feet running up the stairs. She fought to keep control but the last thing she saw was the front door flinging open and the faces of the boys bending over her.

Long minutes before she came to, she had been aware that the room was deserted. Her impressions came hazily but she knew she was alone. Somehow too, she knew she had been out for a while; maybe ten minutes or a quarter of an hour or more. As she struggled to come fully awake she heard a car roaring up the road. Abruptly it stopped at the gate and she heard the car doors slam.

"Jenny!" Thank God, that was Terio.

"Mom!"

"Mom!"

In they came and she tried to rise but all she could do was look at them. Pete and Lis. Herman and Terio. Behind them, the little boy whose name she didn't even know. He was going to tell her but the stick had crashed into the room.

Carefully Terio helped her to sit up and to her it was an enterprise more ungraceful than precarious at the moment.

From that rather absurd concern about her ungainly appearance she knew she had recovered herself.

"The young fellow here used his head," Terio told her. The boy had run out to the street, where he stopped somebody on a motorbike, and the man had gone straight to Mr. Patron's house. "You really did fine, Max," he told the boy, "that was quick action." He said ruefully, "Pete broke one or two rules driving here. But no harm done."

They were relieved but were still looking at her with deep concern, and to her consternation she shed some weak and ragged tears.

In the car she lay back while Pete drove them home, slowly this time. Terio sat up in front with Pete, and looking at Terio's stiff and unrelaxed back she could almost guess his thoughts about stubborn old women, thoughts she was sure he would repeat to her at a suitable time. She still felt light and a little giddy and so, very firmly she decided to take refuge in Terio's thoughts. She told herself: now they were leaving the waterfront and its smell of decaying animals and stagnant water. And she guessed Terio must be thinking, leaving it *for good*. Yet, it was her old home, and home was a formidable thing to withstand corruption—which was always external. Not ever within, not if people, her family, could help it, to the last bit of their sensibilities.

Then it didn't count after all whether the old house was left to fall into ruins or whether Terio would think it worth maintaining. It wasn't a matter of keeping it or not keeping it, anyway, but rather of keeping the quality of the past intact. And so the past in this way was always summoned by the present to commitment and change. The present did change the past in many subtle ways; the little boy Fidel chasing dragonflies was magnified by Fidel the gardener and father of three grown sons; or reduced, if the present's mean spirit should impoverish that past. Here her thoughts somewhat meandered, although still in full stream. And she thought of people, young and old. People who couldn't bear to have their bodies crumble into dust. And yet these bodies did crumble, they always had—even if only for some curious digger to expose the triumphant ruins, after maybe a milennium of their lying in darkness.

She opened her eyes and was a little surprised that the twilight had gone and the stars were there. She lay farther back and watched the constellations wheeling past, wheeling past, it seemed there could be no flickering out, no matter how far one went. ✿

Riverrun

Ninotchka Rosca

Riverrun past Eve and Adam's, from swerve of shore to bend of bay, brings us through a commodious vicous of recirculation, back to Howth's Castle and environs...

Finnegan's Wake — James Joyce

THE KITCHEN clock strikes the hour softly: one, two, three, four, five... before the fourth note is sounded, she has stretched herself midway through a yawn that ends as a sigh. She is up and about, leaving the bedclothes warm with sleep, and steps out into the drowsy morning air. There are the maids to be awakened, the dogs to be led out to the yard, the meals to be cooked, the thousand little details that turn into minutes, into hours, into days. Already, the sunlight is stepping with shy uncertain feet over the boundaries of the night; the pendulum of the clock moves left, right, left, right—an inexorable command.

The maids rise from their *buri* mats stiffly, like yesterday's blossoms forced to greet the sun. They seem forever to carry, in the mornings, the accumulated fatigue of time stretching to their birthbeds. Over here is Lucy and that is Amy and there is Maria; identities sealed only by the difference in their respective heights, a difference blurred over by the sisters' dark skins, squat figures and stumpy legs. Faces remain hidden by black bursts of hair—faces pinched and hidden and bowed over the pot being scrubbed, the floor being waxed, the clothes being washed. They move silently through the house, limbs swift like oiled machines, fed by some invisible current of power, as stern and tenuous as a king's gift of life. They remain vague, shadowy shapes within the rim of her sight as soon as she too trudges through the morning's demands and prepares the day for its beginning.

Very soon, there is a loud step on the stairs, the sound of doors opening, of water raging from the faucets. The two sons wake up at the same time and prepare for school, the daughter is up and striding firmly to the table; the father is in the bathroom, flesh shaken into awareness by the cold shower of water. The moment of exit draws near. She is lost, for this slice of time, between the pieces of bread and the vanishing coffee in the porcelain cups, the tinkle of forks hitting the edges of plates. There is, between the spearing of a bit of food and the opening of a mouth to receive it, little repose for the thought's perambulation.

Then, quite quickly, everything is silent in the house, save for the outside noise of the traffic that has grown suddenly monstrous. The clock strikes the hour irritably: one, two, three, four, five, six, seven, eight. She half-acknowledges the passing of the sun in the sky, the silent roar of its furnace now stoked by the minutes. There is a half-expectant halt in the air; the day cocks its ear and is rewarded by the last sound of the morning's entrances. Two pairs of feet grace down the flight of stairs and the newlyweds enter, eyes still drowned in some dream of bliss, now thinning in the heat of the day.

She prepares their breakfasts, with a maid assisting her. Today, it could be Lucy or Amy or Maria—there is no fixed rule for her favor. but rather that moment of grace is guided by the whim of her internal weather. Coffee, dark and viscous, in white gilded cups; eggs exact and staring in brown-rimmed plates; bread nestled in the folds of immaculate white napkins. The two eat slowly, lingering over the smell of food, lingering over the tastes of the morning's beginnings. Between bites, one would nestle his head on the other's shoulder and steal a second's nap or two, prolonging the communion possible only in sleep. Watching them, she wonders again how it is possible never to have enough time to tell each other of the world's events.

She takes her second cup of coffee for the morning, moving back to the table where the two eat, shyly, with many half-turns and uncertain attempts to regain the isolation of her kitchen. She moves as though in a soft persuading spell. The two, half-roused from the trance of bliss, move apart, eye her with surprise. She sits before them, impelled by some necessity that is barely acknowledged by her submerged mind. Between sips of the liquid, she talks to them, all the while willing herself to cease, to stop, to return to her own agony of silence. But she talks, telling them of the morning's details, the hour's worries. And the two listen politely, staring at her while the eggs grow rigid upon the plates and the lard cements a crusty tomb over them. Is it resentment she spies peeking out of their sleep clogged eyes? No matter, the morning silence seduces her mind into the alleys of remembrance.

Their faces fill the vacuum of her eyes—she peers intently, from behind her rimless glasses, first upon this face and then, the other. The son now; her son. With a jolt she remembers how that young face, now bedewed with sleep, turned hard and agonized: the bushy eyebrows knitted together in pain, the shy lips pursed in anger, the eyes, behind the lowered lids, black with heat. She had hounded him with the whiplash of her voice, from room to room, from corner to corner of this house of her family, until he seemed crazed with the absence of a sanctuary from a mother's wrath. She had clawed at him with her hoarse voice, lashed him with her contempt, flogged him with her piteous cries, until that day when his face had, before her eyes, burst into lightning and his eyes had bored with iron will into her own. "I am a man now, mother," he had said in a choked voice, "a man!" And that had been enough. She had turned away, crushed and defeated, lips sealed upon a heart full of complaint, as half-forgotten lessons of submission revived within her—the legacy of her generation of mothers from generations of women before her, on to the dawn of time upon the world, an unbroken rule of submission to the phallic power and mystery.

He had brought his bride home a few months after that day and seeing him step across the threshold, his arm possessive about this new young waist, she knew that his heart had closed upon heart, he had closed upon her, and now showered the passion of his gaze upon a different face. That night of their homecoming, she had lain in torment, suffocated by the night air that leaned so heavily, so seductively upon the bedclothes held tightly by her listening fingers. It had seemed as though the house would crash down her ears, so heavily, so warmly if the night-air lean upon its walls, its rafters, its ceilings.

Remembering all this, she continues to talk as though the external self of her being had been disconnected from that inner eye that roams upon the vast landscape of memory and time. She takes note of the two pairs of eyes tracing the reality of her voice upon her face. A glance exchanged, the incessant movement of the clock's pendulum, a sigh, a movement—and she knows the morning now proceeds. With a quiver in the heart, she lays down her coffeecup, rises from her chair even as the two stand up to prepare for their step into the outside world. It has been too swift, too sudden in passing.

In other days, other weeks, other months, other years, this hour between the second cup of coffee in the morning and the first sizzle of the frying pan for lunch would be the time for her conversation with her elder sister. She would come in, Consuelo, noisy and fidgety from the long voyage from her husband's province, bearing her week's clothes in an old time-beaten overnight bag. It would always be a big event, this visit, for she comes rarely, unusually, suddenly, without notice, and departs with just the same swiftness for the region where she had been transplanted by a man now long lying in his own region beneath the earth. A moment's rest, and warm bath, and soon the mornings would find the two of them in the shadows of her too-big room, seated in their respective rocking chairs. To and fro, to and fro, the chairs would move and she would allow herself to be lulled, to drift gently to tranquility. Now and then, she would open her beguiled eyes and catch a glimpse of two heads in the overbearing mirror of the dresser. Two heads—one silvery, the other, salt-and-pepper. Despite the twenty years of difference in their ages, the heads in the mirror would seem like twins, as though the skulls had pierced through the deceiving layer of flesh and youth, to reveal their only real fidelity.

Their lips would open, even as their minds open with the rhythmic oscillation, weaving again, from some cobwebbed image of the past, a golden thread of pleasure. Do you remember...? And that time when....? The words drift and float lazily between them; the air is perfumed by familiar and lost scents; yellowing laces bloom into astounding whiteness; the rustle of silk is in the air. Atang de la Rama, surprised by her lover beside the clear brook, stands up, revealing a lithe figure sheathed by a red-patterned *tapis*. The Zorilla rocks, applause and the sudden intake of breath clashing like cymbals in the darkened chamber. She rises, and flings the golden passion of her voice into the air, while her lover, dark-haired and dark-eyed, meets her challenge with a voice deep and vibrating with love.

Love. One finds it in the evenings of carnival and balls, where women swooned over the molten glances of Huseng Batute. Evenings that are of the filigree of lace and the froth of satin, white *dama de noche* and violins from the indifference of the night. The weapons of the hour are extremely perishable: multicolored eyes of beads that very readily lose their lustre; veils looping from beaten silver combs; tender-stalked, lace-woven fans held by ivory fingers at just the right angle.

She holds one now by the fingers of a cold hand, while her nostrils drink deep of the faint scent that perfumes the little breeze the fan raises. She stands beneath a bamboo cornice all darkly green with fern fronds; what terrible frailty is this that she exhibits, laced and powdered and perfumed, this evening of her beginning? And that young man there, all flashing eyes and white teeth, so cocksure, so confident, as he measures the barrier inscribed by her slowly waving fan—does he divine the hushed palpitation, the silent quivering behind the fatal armor of gown, veil and fan? He walks away, throwing lingering glances over his shoulder, his eyes beckoning. What confidence is it that assures him of her obedience? She fixes her eyes upon his shadow and thinks of how very like a woman it is; even in the tiniest of rooms, it follows and will not leave.

ALAS, SHE had followed him, out of that carnival hall into the years and down to the fluid weariness of age! She recalls herself with a jolt while the clock rings the hour in imperious notes: one, two, three, four, five... the chimes echo through the quiet house, full of complaint. She stands from the rocking chair, casts her eyes about the room and prepares to prepare, once more, the little necessities of her day.

Above the sink or over the wave of heat from a stove, her mind closes again, over little half-formed questions: what if I had....? Or if I had....? She stops, frightened by the breathless rush of images from that locked chamber of her being. It happens again and again, she tells herself softly, above the beating of her heart; she has learned never to search too intensely among the unlit corners of her mind; too often, she discovers too many paradoxes, too many ambiguities, too many anagrams for solving. She moves quietly, willing herself to the external world, moving from sink to stove to table and back again.

It takes many hours for the house to be clean again, for the meals to be prepared—and the three maids—Amy, Lucy or Maria—are forever flitting from room to room, constant figures in the periphery of her sight. She talks little, nursing her own aches, and when the pressure bubbles and steams too much for her silence, she lashes out at the maids, her voice crackling above the irascible noise of inaminate things in her world. They are used to her and only half-listen to her words, though she herself is aware of their sting and would prefer to curb her own anger, to lock it in safety somewhere behind a closed door and throw the key to it away. But her sudden, quick explosions clear her chest of suffocating clouds and she is able to go on again, move again, be calm again.

She weeps quietly, painfully, over the stone posts of the house, over the wide windows, the immaculate curtains. She has fought for this, she tells herself, for so many years: fought and schemed and teased and nagged. Why, she asks herself, is the hour of its completion the time for departures? She had treasured its plan through the many difficult years, treasuring it as a tree would keep secret its dream of a piece of earth, valuing it as the country of her life and its extension. Now that it is solid, built as firmly as rock, she finds the tenants of that dream escaped, flown to construct their own dreams. No matter; she has reconciled herself to it, acknowledging the end of a woman's hour—though the doubt and the question remain. Is this to be all, intended to be all, ordained to be all?

She lives with her pain in equanimity, shifting it from side to side in her mind whenever it becomes too much of a burden. It seems it would be the last companion in the house to forsake her side. She keeps silent over it, doing what there is to be done for her family, searching their faces, marking the nearing dawn of the day of their exit. The pain explodes from her only in the rarest of moments, in the garden perhaps when she chances upon that little twig of a guava now grown to a fruit-laden tree; or when those child's eyes suddenly become straight-staring as a man's. Then she would weep quietly, the hot tears scalding her withered cheeks, weep with bitter bitterness over those long years that would never return again.

There remains little time for the dogs' barkings, before the gates clang open, to bring to her that flesh of her flesh now turned stranger from the outside world. She sits heavily, asking for time's mercy, while the pendulum of the clock swings with the abruptness of awareness. The radio is on; she listen with understanding to the magnified pains of other people, other worlds—the melodramatic tragedies, the exaggerated moans, the stretched passions of soap operas. All the sadness of the world seems to fall upon her, and she is consoled by the thought of that rain of tears pouring upon the world.

THAT DARK YOUNG man now, where has he gone to? Portfolio in hand, a bowed old man wipes his feet of the evening's dust and enters her house. He has turned into this graying man who banters with the closing of a life's span, steeling himself against the night with deceptions of youth. During the day, he sits behind a desk, in a small office, playing minor god to the less fortunate, his morals spic and span, his judgment neat and certain. She thinks of him charitably, suddenly remembering how his face would betray him, during those days of their crises, exposing the inner torment he would seek to conceal from her female eyes. He, too, had been reared in a generation of laws and customs; he had breathed the same coded air that had mantled her heart with silence. And that masculine concept had been—still is—as much of a stigmata as the taboos of her sex. In the memory of those days, of his face, she feels the beginning of a tremulous emotion, as though her heart is once more opening to this young man grown gray, after whose figure she had walked like a shadow. They—the two of them—are treading now in the twilight that is not of their own lives merely; they are shades of a generation thinning away, passing away, soon to be shelved in the storeroom of memories and left to the mercy of the years' dust.

How rapidly, she thinks, is this passing! She had seen its knell in the confident steps of her own daughter who strides out of the house each morning to gamble with the world. She sees it now in the tolerance of her own son towards the bride who leaves her first month's marriage bed to forge a separate identity in the external world. Indefinite images of union and cleaving together form in her mind; but she gives no utterance to them; no, not as long as those suddenly too male eyes of her son meet her half-formed sentences with wonder. Instead, she turns to her own generation, to the husband busy with his evening's repast. She sits beside him, in token gesture taking a second bowl of soup while silence lays its chilly hands upon their shoulders.

The clock rings out its note of haste; the day is almost dead, ready for burial. A final flurry of movement in the house marks the moment of its passing. Dishes are to be washed; tables wiped; water to be heated for the day's final ablutions. She walks in and out of the rooms, checking beds, smoothing pillows, preparing the wombs where regeneration proceeds. Tomorrow... ay, tomorrow is another time for struggle, another day for departures, another hour for that further step out of this house she had enshrined in tenuous permanence. In her dark, remaining days, she finds herself beset by doubts, by the uncertainty of right and wrong, by threats to the belief and respect she had held for the legacy of her generation. Her children are growing fast, too fast, it seems, and even now are forging their own legacy, taking little care for comfortable maxims by which her own life had been guided. Confused, she stoops over and straightens an errant pillow upon her husband's bed. At the other corner of the room, her own bed stands ready for her bones.

Is it Amy now or Lucy or Maria who hands her this thin crackling envelope? The piece of paper ignites between her fingers; she peers carefully at the letters that now blur into mistiness, now writhe into cruel clarity. Her knees shake; she feels her limbs turning into water and gropes behind her for a chair. She sinks into it, a sudden sweat upon her brow and a hammering in her chest. White-faced and tight-lipped, she crumples the paper in her hand and secretly slides it into a fold of her dress.

Her husband turns to her with raised eyebrows. Is there anything wrong? She shakes her head forcefully, definitely, though she questions herself about this decision for silence. No, she had not expected it this way, this indecent way with a piece of paper and stranger's hands marking its passage from origin to destination. No, no. Death, she shakes her head, is something intimate, personal; the outsider is sacrilege to it. Shakily, she rises from the chair, and pads about the house in her nightdress, turning the lights out one by one.

IN THE DARK, she hears the quiet sound of her husband's breathing in the other bed. She lies staring into the darkness, ears focused upon that slight sound. She fears intensely its sudden half and the coming of total silence. She listens, not daring to move a finger nor stir a hair and the breath, taking comfort from this silence, goes on its even, rhythmic pace. She lies there in the dark, biting her lips so as not to cry out, while tears begin to sting her eyes.

No, she had not expected it this way; for death to be announced by an informal, scraggy little paper which had passed through who-knew-what hands? She had imagined Death making its own elegant entrance, with a black bordered card as announcement of its presence, with the smell of candles and flowers turning its repulsive reek into mysterious lulling odors. She closes her eyes in a spasm of pity for her sister, now truly a thing of the past and of the earth. Why, she asks herself, is it time for passing into transparence at the moment of union with the concrete earth? She lies, tossing this question in her mind, while her sister rocks slowly, back and forth in the mahogany rocking chair, rocks slowly and contentedly in a secret little room in her mind.

Better, she tells herself, for the end to come crashing now than be tormented with doubts in the last years of one's life. Better to live and pass swiftly now, better for her generation to wither suddenly than to fritter away in inconsequential hours, in insignificant minutes. Better to have had this thread of life cut short long ago than to lie in the December days wondering whether the life that had been lived was really worth the effort of its living. She bites back the thin wail that rises to her throat. In the other corner of the room, the sound of breathing continues undisturbed.

Little by little, the surge of emotion leaves her, drains from her body little by little. Slowly, her mind returns from its upsweep flight; it circles, hovering, above the faces of her days, above the dishes and the meals, the brooms and the dust in the corners, above the little errors that creep unsuspected in a day's motion. She fastens for a moment upon the image of the house's bride, her young face a banner and a challenge both to the past and the present. She had married, this bride, with little thought to others, slashing her own kind of path through the hills of a fresh tomorrow. She, the mother, hovers gently upon her son's face—for that too is both challenge and banner, this generation's own battlecry in the war against yesterday's foibles. She lingers but a moment, sweetly, upon the faces of her children; daughter now enshrined in dreams of her own genesis, the two other sons whose bones stretch and grow eagerly for the hour of their completion.

She leaves these suddenly, quietly, and turns to the days of her slow passing. Ah, those veils, those combs, those fans, those laces, those eyes! She notes suddenly how all that she had taken for beginnings were but the start of a long end, how nearer and nearer to destruction she—and everyone of her own time—had moved in the effort to construct. Smiling with bitterness, she listens to the violins that throb in the evenings of carnivals and balls, while firecrackers ignite the dark into living furious flames. How her feet ache with the many dances of the evening; the trail of her dress is rimmed with the brown stain of dust from the dancefloor. Her eyes flash; her hot tongue moistens those lips now grown tired of smiling. She flees for a moment from the crowd, from the music, to a quiet corner. How thirsty she has become after all those whirls in the arms of young men, all flashing eyes and white teeth! She searches gaily, frantically for a cup of something, a glass of fruitjuice perhaps, while her pounding heart tells her that she thirsts for something more rarified than that, tells her that the burning dryness in her throat can only be cooled by the wine of life.

Slowly, sleep comes to her, the old woman, as she wanders among the tinsel hours of her memories. In the dark, the sound of even breathing is suddenly joined by the chiming of the hours—softly, gently, as though the clock hesitates to rouse the sleeping from the obliteration of the past. One, two, three, four, five, six, seven, eight, nine, ten, eleven... the musical notes fall with hesitancy, teasing the half-awake mind with the hope that the irrevocable is but a turn of the whim, a gesture of the fancy. Sleep drops upon her slowly, dropping like cool fresh water upon her eyelids, upon the skin of her hollowed cheeks, upon the thin arms loosed upon the bedsheets. She feels herself loosed from the moorings of the earth, even as sleep comes swifter and yet swifter, gathering strength, gathering momentum. Her body jerks from its stiffness, her limbs are cast loose upon the waters of this river; sleep pours upon her in a gentle yet powerful current and she is borne off, afloat upon its green waters, out of that bed, out of the room, out of the house and farther still farther to that distance where gleam dully the green tops of great mountains heaved out of the uncharted bosom of an undiscovered earth. ✿

The Writers

1. ESTRELLA D. ALFON, whose first collection of stories won the Commonwealth Literary Contests in 1940, was a well-loved prizewinning fictionist and playwright, an active social worker and columnist in several publications. Seventeen of her stories were published in a collection, *Magnificence and Other Stories*.

2. GILDA CORDERO-FERNANDO, author of a brilliant collection of short stories in *The Butcher, The Baker, The Candlestick Maker* and *A Wilderness of Sweets*, is also a writer for children, a publisher and editor of handsome, lavishly illustrated books.

3. LINDA TY-CASPER, a summa cum laude law graduate of the University of the Philippines, married to critic Leonard Casper, has two daughters and now resides in Boston, where she writes prizewinning novels.

4. AMELIA LAPEÑA-BONIFACIO, University Professor and Director of the CREATIVE WRITING CENTER in the University of the Philippines, dubbed as the "Grand Dame of Southeast Asian Children's Theatre" is playwright-director-designer-storyteller of her well-travelled Teatrong Mulat and founder of the ALB Papet Teatro Museo, both firsts in her country.

5. NORMA O. MIRAFLOR, a prizewinning fictionist and poet who writes bilingually, in Filipino and English, Miraflor's stories have won the *Philippines Free Press*

and the Carlos Palanca literary awards. She is also known as an editor, having edited *Female*, a glossy international magazine in Singapore, where she is now based.

6. KERIMA POLOTAN, a prizewinning short-story writer and novelist and a respected editor, born in the southmost island of Jolo, Sulu, broke all records the year her story, "The Virgin" won two prestigious first prizes, the *Philippines Free Press* Short Story Award and the Carlos Palanca Memorial Award, the same year she gave birth to a set of twins.

7. PAZ LATORENA, born in the colorful town of Boac, Marinduque, received her education in Manila, starting from grade school in Sta. Scholastica and graduating with a degree in Education at the University of the Philippines, where she started writing her well-crafted stories.

8. AIDA RIVERA FORD, fictionist, winner of the Hapwood Award for her first volume of stories, is a director and founder of the FORD INSTITUTE FOR THE ARTS in Davao, where she writes stories, edits a literary journal, conducts workshops, manages a plantation and takes care of an invalid mother and a son.

9. ALBINA P. FERNANDEZ, married to a lawyer-professor and mother of two young lawyers, is a professor in the Department of Filipino and Philippine Literature, University of the Philippines, where she writes her stories and researches on Philippine labor problems.

10. EDITH L. TIEMPO, a prizewinning poet, fictionist and critic, divides time with her novelist-husband, Dr. Edilberto K. Tiempo, between running the Silliman Writers Workshop and visiting poet-daughter, Rowena, who manages the IOWA Writers Workshop at the University of Iowa.

11. CAROLINE S. HAU, a summa cum laude graduate of the Department of English in the University of the Philippines, where she has an appointment as instructor, is currently taking graduate courses in comparative literature in the USA under a Fulbright scholarship grant.

12. NINOTCHKA ROSCA, author of several prizewinning stories is now based in New York City, where she works as freelance writer for major literary magazines and where she receives rave reviews for her novels published by major US publishers.